D1508790

The Road to the Majors

By Scott Blumenthal
and Brett Hodus

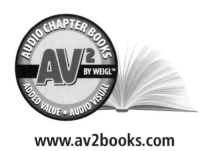

www.av2books.com

Your AV² Media Enhanced book gives you an online audio book, and a self-assessment activity. Log on to www.av2books.com and enter the unique book code from this page to access these special features.

Go to **www.av2books.com**, and enter this book's unique code.

BOOK CODE

D240783

AV² by Weigl brings you media enhanced books that support active learning.

AV² Audio Chapter Book Navigation

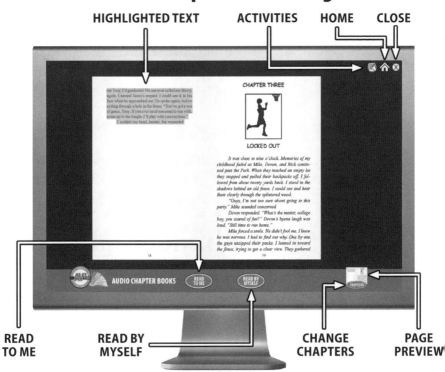

HIGHLIGHTED TEXT ACTIVITIES HOME CLOSE

READ TO ME READ BY MYSELF CHANGE CHAPTERS PAGE PREVIEW

Published by AV² by Weigl
350 5th Avenue, 59th Floor
New York, NY 10118

Website: www.av2books.com   www.weigl.com

First Published by Scobre Educational Press.

Library of Congress Control Number: 2013937477
ISBN 978-1-62127-988-4 (hardcover)
ISBN 978-1-62127-944-0 (single-user eBook)
ISBN 978-1-48960-019-6 (multi-user eBook)

Printed in the United States of America in North Mankato, Minnesota
1 2 3 4 5 6 7 8 9 0   17 16 15 14 13

062013
WEP310513

TABLE OF CONTENTS

Chapter 1   Up, Down, or Out? 4

Chapter 2   A Tough Fall 14

Chapter 3   No Easy Way Out 23

Chapter 4   The Umbrella Man 31

Chapter 5   Back on Track 40

Chapter 6   Blaine Field 46

Chapter 7   Digging a Hole 54

Chapter 8   The Wrong Side of the Fence 60

Chapter 9   It's Just a Game 70

Chapter 10 Getting Up 79

Chapter 11 The Promised Land 85

Chapter 12 Baseball, Without the Perks 95

Chapter 13 The Show 103

Chapter 1: Up, Down, or Out?

I ran in place, kicking up dirt like a lawn mower. I wanted to keep my feet moving. I couldn't play with frozen feet, not today. I looked down at my beat up cleats. They looked worn out next to the bright green grass of the baseball diamond. I was planning on buying a new pair. That morning, I would find out whether or not I could afford them.

"Assignment day" is an important day to a wannabe Major League baseball player. Today, each of us would be placed on a Minor League team or sent home. I'd been awake since 5:00 a.m., wondering where I'd be playing next season.

I ran in place faster. Cold sweat dripped from my forehead onto the soft green grass of Kissimee, Florida. I was twenty-four years old. If I wanted to play in the Majors, I couldn't spend another season in Single A. This spring was the start of my second full season in the Minors. I had to keep moving up.

I started the day by working on my defense. Coach Catta pounded grounders to me at third. The first ball he hit shot off his bat like a rocket. I tried to locate it through the 7:00 a.m. fog. Usually, I'd field the ball cleanly. This one took a strange hop. The grounder hit the edge of the grass and changed direction like a pinball. I dove left and missed. The ball slipped past me.

I pulled my hat down, trying to hide for a moment. Then I punched the center of my mitt. This punch was a signal. "Wake up Jimmy, make this practice count." My glove spent more than a few nights wrapped in rubber bands beneath my pillow. I'd had it since high school. I punched the leather again as a few of the guys arrived at the field. Their nervous looks told me they'd marked "assignment day" on their calendars. We all fought for the chance to play at the highest level. Getting there was the hard part.

The road to the Majors is hardly a smooth ride. A player must first survive Minor League Baseball. Only the very best Minor League players have any chance at reaching the 'big leagues.' These special players must pass through six grueling levels of competitive baseball.

In the Minors, we traveled on buses that smelled like gym class. We slept in hotel rooms that Major Leaguers would use as closets. We lived out of suitcases for months at a time. And we never knew when we would be moved up, down, or out of baseball. We traveled to Shreveport and played double headers in Erie. We played through injuries, and dove on beat up fields. We did all of this every day. And in the end, we all faced the same reality. Some of us would get to the Majors, but most of us would not.

I fielded a few more grounders. Orlando Rodriguez stood at first with his glove extended. I tossed one across the diamond. Orlando yelled at me,

"Hey! Don't pull me off the bag. I don't know what I'm doing out here." Orlando was an outfielder, not a first baseman. I made us both look bad on the next throw. The ball bounced in front of him and skipped into his leg. "You trying to kill me?" He shouted.

I laughed. "You told me not to pull you off the bag. You never said I couldn't hit you."

Orlando moved to my town from Puerto Rico in sixth grade. We'd been playing baseball together ever since. It was great having a friend from another country. I got to learn a lot about his home. Plus, I learned some Spanish from watching so many ballgames with Orlando and his dad.

A few seconds after my poor throw, a voice rang out. "Balance yourself before you make that throw, Hanks." I turned around and saw Bill Putnam, a coach in the Dallas Lonestars organization. The smile left my face. I should have known that someone was watching. Someone was always watching.

The Dallas Lonestars are a Major League franchise. They didn't leave anything to chance. During our time in Florida we were watched closely. Every year Dallas drafts fifty players. Half of them will play Minor League Baseball. For every player who enters the farm system, a player must exit. It's a numbers game that doesn't benefit slow learners.

A few minutes later Benny Catta finished hitting grounders to me. I walked over to Orlando at first base. "Sorry about that throw."

We looked over at our teammates who'd begun stretching. I wondered who among these guys would be going home today. Orlando nudged me. "What do you think?"

I knew exactly what he was talking about. "Double-A, I hope. You?"

Orlando smiled. "I'm going right to the show." The 'show' was the Major Leagues. We both laughed, knowing that neither of us had a shot at that yet. Our next step would be moving past Single A.

The early morning "stretch and catch" was how we loosened up for the day ahead. Usually, this was a time filled with chatter between the guys. We talked about sports and the upcoming baseball season. Everybody had their favorite team and favorite player. Although the friendships were real, so was the competition. We all chased the same dream, a dream that wouldn't come true for most of us.

This was the reason the normal chatter stopped on "assignment day." Today it was too personal. This was a day that we all hated. If not for ourselves, then for the guy whose job we would take at the next level.

We lined up across from one another in the outfield and threw the ball back and forth. I played catch with Chad Barnett, my teammate from Single-A ball. The early morning fog cleared. Baseballs snapped back and forth between partners. A rhythm developed. Somebody coughed, "pop." A bird flew by, "pop." Chad threw a laser that smacked my glove, "pop."

Then, from nowhere, a voice called out. "Bobby Ashbury, you're first." The silence was broken. I recognized Jerry Retskin's strong southern accent. It always got my attention. Jerry and his crew watched Minor Leaguer on top of Minor Leaguer. We all played "catch" together and awaited their judgment. Jerry's crew made the final decision as to which Minor League team we would play on. I believed I'd progressed. I hoped Jerry and his guys thought so too.

One by one, guys entered and exited the clubhouse. There is rarely an expression on a player's face when he returns. Nobody acts too upset or excited. Most guys just got back into line and kept throwing. Others whispered something to a friend. Sometimes a guy would walk right past the line. We'd usually never see or hear from him again.

But most times when guys got cut they tried not to show emotion. Those tears drop later, when you pack up your stuff. The same stuff you packed on road trip after road trip. Only this time you pack for home. You leave the clubhouse one last time to start the rest of your life—a life without baseball. I hoped today wasn't my day to go home.

I noticed Chad Barnett walking back from the clubhouse. He moved slowly but with confidence. I wanted to ask him where he was playing, what had happened, what did Jerry say? I had a million questions. I kept them to myself. I ended up saying, "Hey buddy."

Chad responded, "Hey Jimmy." He let out a small laugh without showing his teeth. I felt relieved.

"Where are you playing?" I quietly asked him.

Chad tried hard to hide his excitement. "Amarillo, Double-A ball, Jimmy."

"Congratulations." We bumped fists. He looked like he was about to say something, but didn't. I understood. There was nothing to say. If I was joining him in Texas, we'd celebrate tonight. If I wasn't, we'd probably never see each other again. There was more than just baseball on the line that day. Friendships were also at stake.

I bent down to tie my shoelace. When I picked my head back up, the sun was in my eyes. I could barely make out the figure of Brian Peterson. He walked quickly back from the clubhouse. "Jimmy, you're up. Hope someone around here gets some good news," Brian avoided my eyes when he spoke.

I made my way toward the locker room. I wanted to get this over with quickly. When I reached the door to Jerry's office I paused before entering. I took a deep breath. The office was poorly lit. A flickering Dallas Lonestars lamp sat on the corner of the desk. "How's it going, Jerry?" I asked as I shook his hand before taking a seat.

Jerry knew me as a laid back California kid. I did my best to keep my cool and lean back in the chair. He reached across his desk and fiddled with the light bulb inside the Lonestars lamp. The room became bright. "Well, I guess I can start by telling you that you are now a member of the Amarillo Dusters." In one sentence I'd received my promotion. Jerry smiled. I smiled back. After one season at the Single-A level, I was moving up to Double-A. I was through leaning back in my chair at this point. Jerry broke in with his southern accent, "Congratulations on that accomplishment. The jump from A ball to Double-A is a real important one." I was speechless.

I shook Jerry's hand and left the clubhouse. I was going to Double-A Amarillo! I was moving to Texas. I was two steps away from the Majors. I was closing in on my dream faster than expected. I was hitting and fielding better than ever. Life was great.

Practice came to a close. I was showered, dressed, and out of there before half the guys left the field. Hector Gomez stood behind me in the parking lot. "Hey Jimmy, congratulations." Hector and I had both been promoted to Amarillo. "Thanks, man," I said. "You too."

I hopped into my car and Hector banged on the window. I rolled it down. "What's up?" I said.

Hector smiled, "Do you know where Amarillo is?"

I smiled back, shrugged my shoulders and drove away. I had no idea where Amarillo was. But I did know that it was one step closer to my dream.

After practice, I drove back to the apartment

I'd been renting with Orlando. On the ride over, I blasted the radio. I can't remember what song was on, but it fit my mood perfectly.

Orlando and I sat in the living room. We were excited about what had happened that day. We were laughing and were louder than usual. After a few minutes Orlando asked me the question I'd been thinking about for an hour. "You wanna surf before the sun goes down?" He didn't have to ask twice. We grew up together in Southern California. And although baseball was my life's passion, surfing wasn't too far behind it.

In our time in Florida, Orlando and I met two girls who became our surfing buddies. Jen grew up in Florida and Maria was born in Cuba. They were excellent surfers and big baseball fans, too.

Orlando called the girls. Fifteen minutes later we were heading to the beach. We pulled up just as the sun was starting to set. The girls were already in the water. Orlando called out to them, "How'd you get here so quick?"

Maria laughed, "You baseball players are slow."

Orlando smiled. "No, Jimmy's slow. I've got six stolen bases this spring already."

With that comment I jumped into the water. "Faster than you," I yelled to Orlando. I fought my way out past the break. The waves crashed in on me. These were some of the biggest I'd seen.

Surfing in Florida was different than surfing out west. It wasn't the size or shape of the waves. It was more the way the water looked. Growing up in Southern California had spoiled me. I was used to clear blue water. In Florida, the water was a muddy brown. This made it hard to judge depth. Crashing into shallow water was a sure way to get hurt. I'd just received a promotion to Double-A ball. The last thing I needed was an injury.

I rode my first wave on Jen's heels. She'd competed as a pro surfer, so following her was always a smart move. Her board seemed to be in tune with the ocean and her timing was incredible. I leaned in too much and crashed into the cool water. I watched Orlando crash and burn on the same wave. Maria and Jen laughed as they hopped off at the end of their ride. These girls could surf.

We spent the next thirty minutes riding one large wave after another. Orlando and I were equals in terms of surfing. And just like in baseball, we competed hard against one another. The girls were done for the day. They sat on the shore, toweling off. Orlando and I were side by side on our boards. We waited for the last ride of the night. "I can't believe we're going to Double-A," I said.

"One step closer, Jimmy."

"One big step," I answered.

We made eye contact and then there was silence. We both quietly thought about the next step in *our lives. And then we saw it—the biggest wave of the day. Right away, I started paddling and so did Orlando. Neither one of us wanted to miss this one.*

I felt it coming from fifty yards back. The ocean seemed to rise a few feet for this monster. My heart started to beat quicker and my arms paddled. "Here we go!" I yelled to Orlando as I jumped up onto my board. The power of the ocean rushed me toward the shore. The wind blew hard and I crouched down, rising higher and higher. The wave picked up more and more steam. I was traveling faster than I'd ever traveled before. And that's when I felt that something wasn't quite right. My balance gave way and I started to wobble toward a headfirst crash.

The next thing I knew I was beneath the water. My body was thrashing hard into the ground. My head smacked the ocean floor with a thud. The swirling water pushed me back toward the surface. I was out of breath and in pain. I could see that my head was bleeding. I was looking for Orlando, Jen or Maria, but I couldn't see them. I was dazed. I couldn't tell which way the shore was. And I didn't even have time to take a deep breath before another wave crashed over my head. And then I was numb.

My eyes closed and memories began to flash through my head. I remembered that before surfing, before baseball, before spring training, college, or the Minor Leagues, I was a soccer player...

Chapter 2: A Tough Fall

It's funny the things you remember at the strangest times in your life. Giant waves crashed over me and all I could picture was my mother. She was standing in our kitchen making peanut butter sandwiches. We lived in a suburb of San Diego called Oceantown. Dad worked close by, and we loved the beach. By the time I was twelve, I spent a lot of my time surfing. The rest of my time was spent playing baseball, basketball, and soccer.

"Jimmy, can you bring this up to your room? I don't want your smelly soccer bag sitting in my kitchen." She cut my sandwich in half. "Now please." Mom's voice demanded action.

I picked up my bag from the floor. Then I ran upstairs, throwing it into my room. A soccer ball rolled out onto the floor. I tapped it around with my feet. I loved kicking that ball. I heard my mother's voice again. "Lunch is ready. Stop kicking the ball in the house." I placed it back in the bag and walked down the stairs.

I was pretty good at surfing, baseball, and basketball, but soccer was my passion when I was twelve. I used to practice with Danny Stevenson, my best friend at the time. One day after school, we were kicking the ball around at the field up the street. Danny was confident with his right foot. "Go back a few steps. Farther. Move back like ten more feet. I want to air this one out." Danny always challenged himself. I ran back to about thirty yards away. To my surprise, he booted one over my head.

I sprinted to run the ball down. During my dash, I tripped and fell. "Jimmy? You OK?" Danny looked concerned. Really, I think he just wanted to kick the ball again. "Tough fall," Danny said. He chased down the soccer ball and began juggling it. He wanted to get started again.

I looked at the grass stains on the front of my shirt. It was a shirt I took great pride in wearing. "My San Diego University shirt," I groaned. I slid my fingers toward a hole in the fabric. I felt my bare skin and looked up at Danny, "I ripped my shirt." I was upset.

Danny thought he could solve my problem. "Don't worry, Jimmy, I've got an extra shirt." He ran to get his soccer bag.

A few moments later, Danny was back, dribbling the ball in a zigzag motion. I forgot about my shirt. My eyes were drawn to his Tidal Waves bag. The Tidal Waves were an elite group of soccer players from the San Diego area. This wasn't the first time I'd admired that bag. I liked the strange light blue color. And the huge wave that crashed over the words "BAYSIDE TIDAL WAVES" was cool too. I wanted one of those bags. I wanted to be a Tidal Wave.

Excitement pumped through my body. I got to my feet and stole the ball from Danny. I dribbled down toward a tree that we had marked as the goal. He followed me closely. We raced for about fifty yards. I could feel him on my heels. I thought about the tryouts that would take place in a few months. I knew I would need to get faster and stronger.

I was ten yards from the tree when I had enough room for a shot. I swung my leg back, ready to fire. An instant before I made contact, Danny slid in from behind me. He knocked the ball away. Now he was the one dribbling. He reared back and shot a bullet that smacked the tree. "Goal!" Danny shouted. "Goal!"

I hung my head. "Nice play," I said without looking at him. I tried to catch my breath, but I was beaten. Danny sat down on the grass. I followed his lead. "When are tryouts for the Waves again?" I always asked this question.

"I've told you ten times, Jimmy. They're during baseball season, first week of April."

The first week of April finally rolled around. Danny and I had to go to baseball practice on the day of tryouts. My mind couldn't focus on baseball. I played terribly. We left early to make sure we didn't miss the tryout. We were hazed by our teammates for our early exit.

Doug Bird, a scrawny guy with a big mouth, had to get in the last word. "Soccer's more important than baseball, huh Jimmy? We don't need you anyway," he laughed at his own joke. Doug was right, soccer was more important to me than baseball.

We arrived at the tryout and stepped out of my mother's car without speaking. Danny and I walked onto the choppy grass together. There were lots of guys trying out for the Tidal Waves. They all looked bigger and stronger than me. The field, like most fields I'd played on, was in bad shape. The torn-up grass covered a bumpy ground that was covered with small rocks. The out-of-bounds lines were faded and the goals were tangled and torn.

I walked over to the sidelines to put on my shin guards. Danny sat next to me. All of the guys from last year's team stood in a row. They guarded the field like a gate. I hoped none of them noticed me. When I glanced up, all of the elder Tidal Waves were staring at me. They knew who I was. Danny must have told them about me.

One of the bigger guys waved in my direction. I gave a small nod, thinking he was waving at me. I thought wrong. A moment later, Danny waved back and stood up. He joined his teammates.

Ten minutes later, Danny came over to talk to me. "How ya feeling?"

I looked back at him and tried to sound confident. "Pretty good."

Danny didn't look convinced. He patted me on the back. "Don't worry so much. Come over and meet the guys. It'll be good for you to get to know everyone before practice starts."

I thought meeting the guys was a good idea. But my body didn't seem to agree. My throat sunk into my stomach and talking became difficult. I was nervous. We walked towards them and Danny introduced me. There were seven returning Tidal Waves. This left seven spots open to the rest of us. I stood uncomfortably in front of the guys. I heard a few snickers. A few guys ignored me. And the rest of them just stared.

Danny introduced me. "Guys, this is my friend Jimmy from Oceantown. Let's make sure we get him the ball today." Danny had spoken, but everyone just kept staring.

Then a big guy with whiskers on his upper lip chimed in. "From Oceantown, huh?"

I tried to be friendly. "Yeah, I—"

He cut me off. "Are you a surfer?"

I didn't want to answer this question. I did anyway. "Sure, I surf, but I play soccer and base—"

He cut me off again. "Yeah, you're definitely a surfer. You got that wavy hair and everything…dude."

Most of the guys who were on the team were from Bayside. I was from Oceantown—a surf town. So I already had one strike against me. All of the guys started to laugh at my hair. I knew it was time to walk away. This exchange made me even more determined. I would show them that the "surfer dude" could do more than ride waves.

Practice began and we were each assigned to a

team of seven. I was positioned at left forward. On the first exchange, the center on our team nudged me the ball. His kick hit the instep of my right foot. I pushed up the field as fast as I could. I dribbled to the outside and passed the first defender easily. I think my speed caught him off guard. I still had two guys left to beat before I could line up a shot on goal.

The two guys were ready for me. The goalie was ready too. He began to move around, bending his knees and spreading his arms. The first defender slid at me. But I was able to float a pass over his head. The ball landed softly in front of me and I kept dribbling. Now I had everyone's attention. There was only one man left to beat.

The next defender was coming straight at me. I touched the ball with the inside of my left cleat as he charged. After avoiding his slide, I was past him with the ball in front of my right foot. It was me against the goalie. I decided to show off my power. I dribbled twice more and drilled a twenty footer. My blast left the goalie frozen. The ball bounced around in the left corner of the ragged net like a flopping fish.

I had scored on the first play of Tidal Waves tryouts. The "surfer dude" was flashing his skills. But my excitement didn't last. "Hey, let's pass the ball out here. Play as a team!" The angry voice ended my victory parade. I looked toward the sideline and saw Coach Custis. He was exactly like Danny had said. His shiny bald head was half-covered by a Tidal Waves hat. I knew he was speaking directly to me because no one else had touched the ball.

Coach Custis scared me straight. I started passing every time I put my foot on the ball. I lost my confidence. The bigger guys started to make me pay the price. A monstrous halfback ran over me like a runaway train on one play. I was floored. I thought I'd broken my ribs.

Danny came over to help me. "You OK, Jimmy?" I nodded. "Good, then start playing, man!" For some reason Danny's comment woke me up. I remembered that I was actually good at this game. I jumped to my feet and got back into the flow. My confidence grew when I dropped a few nice passes to my teammates.

By the time practice ended, I was exhausted. I collapsed onto the sidelines. The big guy who'd hazed me about my hair earlier, called out to me. "You played good out there," he said. "You've got a shot to make the team." I smiled. I was starting to feel like a Tidal Wave.

That night I made lists of different players who could be chosen for the Tidal Waves. Fourteen guys would make the team. When I made my lists, I was never farther down than ninth. I was confident that Coach Custis would have good news for me when he called.

I got home from school the next day and ran into the house at full speed. The phone call would be between 4:30 and 5:00 p.m. that night. This was perfect because I had soccer practice for my indoor team at 6:00. I stared at the clock in our kitchen nervously. It was 4:30. I tapped my foot against the floor. I must have had six glasses of water. I looked at the clock again, 4:44. I waited and waited. Sure enough the phone rang at 4:59. I picked up the receiver on the first ring.

"This is Coach Custis from the Tidal Waves."

"How's it going, Coach?" I was trying to sound confident.

"Well, I actually called to tell you that we don't have a spot for you this year. I'm sorry it didn't work out." Just like that, I was cut from the Tidal Waves.

"Alright, Coach," I tried to fight back tears. "Thanks for letting me try out."

He could tell that I was upset. "There's always next year, son. Best of luck with your soccer."

I slammed down the telephone and sunk into the chair. What happened? I didn't understand. I began to search for reasons why I'd been cut. If only I would have passed more at the beginning. No, if I would have been more aggressive. Mom walked into the kitchen. She gave me a hug and poured me a glass of milk.

I knew I was going to have to watch Danny carry around his Tidal Waves bag for another year. But I made an important decision that night. I would get my Tidal Waves bag next year. I wouldn't quit.

I had soccer practice with my indoor team in a

half-hour. My friends would definitely ask about try-outs. I'd have to tell them I got cut. I stared out the window blankly. Then Mom asked me the question I had been asking myself for the past few minutes. "What do you want to do about indoor practice? You can stay home if you want, Jimmy." She had never offered me that option before. My parents always taught me that "If you play on a team, you always go to practice."

I paused for a second and wiped a tear from my face. "I want to go, Mom. I'm gonna have to see these guys some time."

I arrived at soccer practice a few minutes early.

Right away, Justin sprinted over to talk to me. "You make the Waves, Jimmy?" I collected myself and tried to smile. "No, I got cut," I said. For a moment, I thought I'd made the wrong choice by coming to practice. "What? How did *you* get cut? You were awesome."

"I don't know," I responded.

"Don't worry, I got cut too." He smiled and we walked to the field together without our Tidal Waves bags.

Chapter 3: No Easy Way Out

I was underwater. That much was certain. Still, I was confused. My mind and body were in a fog. I knew that my board was gone. I'd wrapped the string around my ankle, but somehow, it loosened.

I remembered the first wave clearly— that was the one I rode in. I'm pretty sure that was the big one. That was when I hit my head. I could feel a pounding pain above my left eye. I was cut, but had no way of knowing how badly. Maria, Jen, and Orlando were probably looking for me right now.

The power of the ocean was shifting and twisting my body against its will. There was nothing I could do to stop it. I tried to swim but my arms would barely move. Each time I felt the air, another wave would crash down on me.

I'd spent my entire life running, jumping, kicking, shooting, and sliding. As an athlete, my body had always performed. But now I was fighting against a force greater than an 0-2 fastball. And my body was letting me down.

I started to think about all the times I'd been surfing with my dad and my brothers. I'd always get caught under the waves. I was scared then, too. At least I knew my family was with me...

Whenever we went out to dinner, Dad would make friends with our waiter or waitress. That night was no different. When the waitress approached the table, Dad had her smiling right away. She knelt down next to him like they were best friends. She even pointed out her favorite menu items.

Dad does that to people. The first time you meet him, you feel like you've known him forever. I was proud that he was my father. That doesn't mean I always agreed with him. I remember one decision he made before my freshman year that I couldn't figure out. Dad decided to send me to Bayside High instead of Oceantown Union High. My friends were at Oceantown, so I wasn't happy with Dad's decision.

The only thing I had going for me was that I'd recently become a Tidal Wave. I made the team on my second attempt. A few guys on that team would be starting high school at Bayside too. Still, I was fright ened to be a fourteen-year-old freshman at a new school. "Why can't I just go to school where my friends are? Guys from Bayside don't like guys from Oceantown, Dad. It's not too late to transfer."

"The easy way out" was not part of Dad's vo-cabulary. He stared across the table at me. "Oceantown's a small place, Jimmy. Everyone you know is from here. I expect you to do great things at Bayside."

Dad put his foot down. I had no choice but to face his challenge. "I guess I'll make the best of it. I'll go to Bayside. I just hope I can make some friends."

A surfer boy in an athlete's town, I knew I was

in for some trouble. But I wasn't your average "surfer boy." Sure, I had blonde hair and said words like "dude" and "bro." But I had a good jump shot too. And I could always hit a baseball farther than my friends. The Bayside guys might not be my buddies right away. But they'd have to accept me as an athlete eventually.

I arrived at Bayside for my first day of high school. I was sure there would be plenty of "first-day hazing." I knew the surfer look was not a real popular one. But I didn't want to cut my hair or change the way I dressed. I decided to be myself.

I walked through the double doors at the front entrance of the school. My heart was beating through my shirt. I moved through the large lobby quickly. Right away, a few guys looked over at me. They were tall, muscular, and wore varsity letters on their jackets. I gave the guy in the middle a friendly nod. He wore a pair of dark sunglasses and had a girl hanging from his arm. He led his crew over to me.

"Hey surfer bro, looks like you made the wrong turn. The beach is that way." He pointed to the girls' bathroom and laughed. "We play real sports at this school. So why don't you grab your surfboard and go back to Oceantown." His buddies all stood around him and laughed. He wasn't finished. "Nice hair, maybe I should dye my hair blonde and grow it sideways. Then I can look as stupid as you do." They all started cracking up. Maybe it was time for a haircut, I thought.

I faked a smile and walked away from the guys. I tried to pretend I wasn't rattled. I think it was obvious that I was. Just before I turned the corner, I glanced over my shoulder. The name "Garrett" popped out at me. It was written across the back of the jerk's letterman jacket. There was a baseball bat stenciled on the back. I was sure we'd meet again.

I suffered through a rough first couple days of school. I heard the "surfer boy" jokes and comments about my hair and clothes. But I tried to erase that stereotype through sports.

I always thought soccer would be my sport. But oddly enough, I received more attention on the basketball court than the soccer field. Despite being cut from the Tidal Waves when I was thirteen, I made the team the next year. Though I made the Waves, I was hardly a part of the team. Game after game, I learned how to warm benches with the best of them. So I turned my attention toward a new sport—basketball.

I thought basketball was the answer. That year, I played on the junior varsity team as a freshman. Every day, before anyone showed up at the gym, I would be shooting three pointers. I ran around like a madman. I grabbed rebound after rebound and threw up shot after shot. I loved playing basketball. But I was a one hundred and fifty pound pile of bones. I didn't have the body to be the player I wanted to be. Still, basketball earned me the respect of the athletes at school.

All but one of them. I would have to face him on the baseball field.

My success on the freshman baseball team caught the attention of Coach Edmonds, the varsity coach. Between my freshman and sophomore year I was invited to play summer baseball on his team. An impressive performance during those months would give me a chance to make varsity as a sophomore.

During the practices leading up to our first game Tony Garrett made my life miserable. He was always firing cheap shots at me. Some of the older guys jumped in too. I was one of the younger guys on the team. I carried the equipment from the bus to the field. While my teammates warmed up, I filled up cups of water. I received more than a few wedgies.

I remember the nerves I felt during my first game of summer ball against the Valley Vikings. I had no idea if I would be able to compete at the varsity level. I watched the opposing pitcher warm up on the other side of the field. I stared at him as he threw the fastest pitches I'd ever seen. I continued to look until I heard a familiar voice. "Hanks, are you here to play ball or take a pitch count?" I turned around and saw Tony Garrett. I looked away and jogged to the dugout to get my glove.

When I returned to the field, I paired up with Corey Dunn. He was one of my friends on the team. We warmed up by tossing the ball around the outfield. I tried to show Corey my slider. We were interrupted as a ball flew past my face. I jumped backwards and fell to the ground.

"Oh, my fault," Garrett spoke sarcastically.

I stood up and threw the ball back to him as hard as I could. He caught it and glared at me. "Hey Hanks, do you think you're ever gonna be a part of this team? Right now, you're more like our surfer mascot than our left fielder." This guy never stopped. But he *was* the team captain. So I would have to put up with his words until I earned his respect.

To my surprise, Coach Edmonds let me know that I was going to pitch a few innings today. I guess I got in there because I could throw hard. I received an early call to the mound when our starting pitcher was lit up for six runs in the first inning.

As I warmed up, I felt confident. I was throwing hard and hitting my spots. No one touched base during my first inning. I was actually feeling pretty good. That is, until Frank Silvano stepped into the batter's box in the third. The stocky Valley Viking rocked my first offering up the middle. His single put him on first with nobody out. After I threw a wild pitch to the next batter, Silvano was in scoring position at second.

The next batter singled, and Silvano tried to score. A perfect toss from right field arrived in Kyle Wicks' glove after just one bounce. Kyle caught the ball and waited to apply the tag. Silvano was going to be out by about five feet. Instead of slowing up, he slid into home plate with his cleats high. Wicks tagged him out easily, but paid the price.

The two players tumbled over one another as Silvano's spikes ripped through Kyle's pants. He tore a large patch of unprotected skin stretching six inches across Kyle's thigh. A stream of blood came pouring down his leg. He had to be carried off the field. It was the grossest thing I'd ever seen on a baseball field.

Silvano only received a warning from the umpire and remained in the game. Our team was very upset. After the inning ended, Tony Garrett pulled me aside in the dugout. His word on the diamond was much like Coach's. I listened closely. I knew he wouldn't let Silvano get away with that slide.

Tony grabbed me by the collar of my shirt and pulled me close to his face. I could taste his lunch. "When Silvano comes up again, I want you to hit him with a fastball. Nobody gets away with that garbage!" I listened to what Tony was saying. I thought carefully about his words. But I didn't want to throw at anyone. Garrett saw my discomfort. He knew I wasn't on board with his plan. "If you want to be a part of this team, then prove it." He slammed a baseball down hard into the center of my mitt.

I was hoping that Coach would pull me out of the game before Silvano came to the plate. I didn't want to deal with the situation. I moved steadily through the order. Nobody was warming up in our bullpen. Coach had no intention of pulling me. Silvano stood in the on-deck circle. I was going to have to pitch to him.

This left me with a difficult decision. If I didn't throw at Silvano, I might never have another chance to gain the respect of Tony Garrett. Part of me felt like Silvano deserved a fastball in his side. The other part of me didn't want to be the guy to deliver the pitch. There was no easy way out.

Silvano came to home plate and I made a huge mistake. I turned and looked right at Tony. He was pacing back and forth, kicking up dirt. He stared at me. I knew what I had to do. My control was great that day. I was sure I would be able to hit Silvano's leg with a fastball. The knockdown would serve as payback for what he'd done to Kyle. I hoped this would get Tony off my case once and for all.

I took the sign from our new catcher, and nodded in approval. I wound up and tossed the ball toward home plate. The pitch headed right for Silvano's midsection. He attempted to get out of the way but it was too late. The ball smacked him in the hip.

Silvano fired his bat to the dirt. I knew he was in some pain and I felt bad. Not as bad as I felt for Kyle, though. The umpire threw me back another baseball. He gave me a warning too. I took a deep breath and turned to look at Tony. He nodded his head and touched the bill of his cap. His days of hazing me had come to an end.

Chapter 4: The Umbrella Man

The ocean was giving me all I could handle and I was fighting it. For the first time in awhile, I was moving in the direction I was pushing. This was a good thing.

Suddenly, the haze that had cast over me was lifted. I realized that if I moved in the same direction long enough, I would find the air or the ground. I kicked my feet and swung my arms until my face hit something solid. I'd found the ground.

With the waves continuing to crash above me I pushed off the ground as hard as I could. I now knew which way was up. With my eyes closed, I continued to push. And then I felt wind on my head. I quickly gasped for air. But my relief was short lived. When I opened my eyes I saw another wave about to crash on me.

"Jimmy? Jimmy, can you hear me?" I heard Orlando screaming my name in the distance. This meant he was looking for me.

I tried to raise my hand up but the next wave came down on me harder than any of the others. Then there was blackness again. Just hearing one word out of Orlando's mouth made me remember a thousand conversations we'd had. I recalled one talk we had when I was fifteen. That conversation changed my life. Orlando was the first person who ever called me a ballplayer...

"I know you love basketball, Jimmy. But I don't understand why you don't just concentrate on baseball. You could be awesome." Orlando told me this as we sat on my couch playing video games. I gave him a strange look and scored a goal. He pretended not to notice that I'd scored. "All I'm saying is that basketball's a waste of time. It's not like you're going to play in the NBA." He spoke loudly

I knew I wasn't going to be a professional basketball player. That wasn't why I started playing in the first place. "I'm not trying to get to the NBA or the Majors. I just love playing both sports." I told Orlando.

"I saw you play basketball this season, and you were good. But think about baseball. You made varsity during summer ball after your freshman year! If we practice hard, we could take this all the way. Imagine that? Jimmy Hanks and Orlando Rodriguez, Major League ballplayers!" His face lit up as he confessed his dream to me.

I stared at him blankly. "Yeah right, O."

I didn't admit it, but listening to Orlando changed the way I approached my future. Maybe I did have a chance. I shut off the video game and moved into the kitchen. Orlando had got me thinking.

I responded to his comments with the greatest weapon I had against him, logic. "You know, we have like a one-in-a-million chance at playing sports for a living. Seriously O, I like the odds of a college education much better." I wasn't finished. "I'm gonna go to San Diego University. That's my plan. I'll study hard there, and then I'll be a banker like my dad."

I loved playing sports more than anyone. But I knew that I had a better chance of becoming an astronaut than a ballplayer. So I dreamed quietly. The days and nights passed. And soon, my dreams were all about baseball. Even in my sleep I was plotting my road to the Majors.

Every day, Orlando's words echoed in my head. "Imagine that, Jimmy Hanks, a Major League Baseball player?" I did imagine. As my junior year rolled around, I started wondering if basketball was worth my time.

After a strong sophomore season in which I batted .328, I was sure some college would notice me—too sure. The pressure I put on myself weighed on me. I lost my confidence more with each out I made. My average during my junior season was around .260 and I couldn't figure out what was wrong.

Still, our team managed to make the playoffs. Our first-round game was against Kingston High School. The Southern California sky was gray that day. Fog had rolled into the outfield. The layers of white were so thick that I could barely see the pitcher's mound. Only a few damp fans were still in the stands. A light rain had scared the rest away. I walked into the dugout and sat on the bench next to Orlando. He was staring into the bleachers. "You believe that fog?"

As usual, Orlando was in his own world. "What?"

I noticed him staring into the stands. "Are you looking for someone?"

"Nope. Just hoping someone's looking for me." Orlando pointed into the stands. "Let's see, we've got the assistant coach from the University of Long Beach. And to his right are two Major League scouts." These were the people we had to impress in order to reach the next levels of competitive baseball.

I noticed a few faces Orlando hadn't mentioned. "Who are those two guys behind my mom?"

He leaned his head forward. "Which guys?"

I pointed to the two men I was talking about. They sat a few feet apart from one another. I wasn't sure if they knew each other. "That guy on the left might be wearing a San Diego University jacket. And who's that guy with the huge umbrella?"

"Every guy wearing blue isn't an SDU coach, Jimmy." Orlando replied.

I guess I was obsessed with the Sharks. Orlando stood up to get a closer look. "I don't know who those guys are."

We took some infield practice before the game started. Standing at third base, I fielded ground balls. In between throws to first, I scanned the bleachers. I was looking to see if the man with the blue jacket *was* an SDU recruiter. Mom clapped her hands in front of the man in question. I gave her a smile. Then I made a nice backhanded stop off the bat of Coach Custis. I fired the ball across the diamond. There was that royal blue baseball jacket again.

Coach hit me another grounder. I fielded it cleanly, but the muddy ball slipped through my fingers. My throw sailed high above the head of our first baseman. My focus was lost. I peered over again. My mother was gone. The rain had picked up a little and I guess she'd gone home. I now had a clear view at the man in blue. I was right all along. The man wearing the jacket was Larry Diaz, the assistant baseball coach at San Diego University. I had been attending SDU games since I was a little kid and recognized him.

I quickly looked away, fielded a tough grounder and made a strong throw to first. After the play, I noticed Mr. Diaz speaking with the "umbrella man." I wondered if the owner of the umbrella was affiliated with SDU as well. I ignored this question. It was time to focus on baseball.

Kingston opened the scoring with six runs in the first four innings. The cold air didn't chill their hot bats. It had certainly cooled ours, though. By the time we came to the plate in the bottom of the fourth, we trailed 6-0. We were twelve outs away from a long off-season. With our season on the line, Tony Garrett came to the plate. He swung at an 0-1 fastball and drilled one over the shortstop's head.

Orlando followed Tony's lead, lacing a double

into the right field corner. Our bats had come alive. Suddenly, our entire team was making noise.

There were runners on second and third when I walked to the plate. I glanced over my shoulder. Larry Diaz and his umbrella-toting friend were standing. I dug into the batter's box, staring at my grip. The first two pitches were low and outside. I was looking for a pitch that I could drive. If it wasn't perfect, I didn't need to swing.

The next offering was perfect—a belt-high fastball. I teed off, cranking one to left field. The ball easily cleared the outfield fence. My home run chopped Kingston's lead in half. Kingston 6, Bayside 3.

That hit changed the game. We started playing better after shrinking the lead. When I came to bat in the bottom of the sixth, we trailed by only one. The tying run was on third base with one out. All I needed was a deep fly ball. Our playoff lives were resting on my bony shoulders.

The first pitch was a curve ball over the outside corner, strike one. I had been looking for a fastball. The off-speed pitch really fooled me. The next pitch was a low fastball that I golfed to left field. I knew as soon as I made contact that I'd hit one deep enough to tie the game. I sprinted toward first base as the left fielder moved under the ball. He began fading toward the wall. He was waiting for my deep fly to land in his glove. He began running out of room. When I saw his back slam against the fence, I knew I'd hit another homer.

I pumped my fist high in the air as I crossed home plate. Bayside 7, Kingston 6. Game over. My teammates slapped the top of my helmet in excitement. Even Tony Garrett, my old enemy, joined. Orlando slapped my head hard enough to make my ears ring. "I told you that you were a ballplayer, didn't I?" He was right. I was a ballplayer. I only hoped that Larry Diaz thought so too.

I walked over to the dugout to get my gear and go home. I was taking off my cleats when I noticed Larry Diaz. He was stepping into our dugout. I wondered if he was coming in to talk to me. My heart raced. I jumped up, excited to greet him. As he walked down the steps, I imagined myself in an SDU uniform. I had been waiting years for this moment. He reached out to shake my hand, "Heck of a game, Jimmy."

I was nervous, "Thank you sir, I..."

"Oh, there's Silver, right there." He pointed to the end of the bench. Jake Silver, our star pitcher, was picking the mud from his cleats. Mr. Diaz patted me on the shoulder and moved past me. He had come to see Silver, not me. I quickly fired everything into my baseball bag. I hurried barefoot out of the dugout. Two home runs— one, a game winner, and all I got was a pat on the back.

Jake Silver sat with Larry Diaz. The two joked around like old friends.

I walked to the parking lot alone. I tried not to be upset. I had just played the game of my life. So how come nobody cared? As this thought entered my head, the floodgates opened. Rain soaked my cap, my clothes, and my spirit. I wanted to go home.

A voice came from nowhere. "You always walk barefoot in the rain?" I looked up and noticed the "umbrella-man" leaning against the side of my truck. Who was this guy? Despite his friendly smile, I still had a bad taste in my mouth from Larry Diaz. "Can I help you with something?" I snapped.

"Maybe I can help you. Get under this umbrella." I noticed a Major League logo on the man's umbrella. I moved underneath it. The "umbrella man" was a tall, well-built, African American man in his early thirties. He extended his large hand with a smile. "Well Jimmy, Coach Edmonds has a lot of good things to say about you. I'm Roger Davie, a scout for Seattle. It's nice to meet you." I was shocked that the stranger knew who I was.

This was the first Major League scout I'd ever met in person. I wasn't sure exactly what I was supposed to say. My voice was shaky. "Nice to meet you, sir."

"I scout the West Coast for Seattle. I came here today to take a look at Orlando Rodriguez. He's a fine ballplayer."

I was happy for Orlando. But was I about to get overlooked again? "He sure is. He's a great guy too," I said.

Mr. Davie kicked water from a large puddle that had formed around my truck. "To tell you the truth, Jimmy, I was impressed with you. I think you swing a mature bat. I don't see patience in a high school hitter too often." This was unbelievable. I must have said "thank you" five times. He continued, "Keep it up. Who knows, you could be a draft pick this June." Me? A draft pick? Just thinking about playing Minor League baseball was exciting.

I had to say something. "Mr. Davie, I don't know what to say." That was all I could come up with.

Roger reached into his back pocket and pulled out an index card with a Seattle logo in the corner. He laughed, sensing my excitement. "Just keep up with your schoolwork and keep playing as hard as you can. And here," he handed me the card, "try to keep this dry. We'll be in touch."

Chapter 5: Back on Track

I was beneath the water again and my body was tired and beaten. I began to space out. I wasn't listening for Orlando's voice anymore. For a few seconds, I wasn't really there. I could hear the waves crashing above me. The sounds started to form patterns. Soon, I was lost.

I began to remember random moments of my life. In kindergarten, I was rolling toy trucks through the sandbox. My friend Doug Bird was smiling the way he did years later on the baseball field. I remembered drinking hot chocolate at the top of the ski slope with Dad. Then I was nine years old, standing up for the first time on my surfboard. My board was blue and carried me like I was walking on water. I felt like I was actually there.

I remembered driving my old black pickup. I'd just gotten my driver's license. When I came home, my friends were all waiting for me. We fit about six of us into my truck. Then we drove over to Big-Bite Burgers and stuffed ourselves until we were sick. The scene was so real. I could almost taste the burgers and hear the laughter.

And then I started to remember the long road I traveled on to get to the Minors. There were a thousand memories that led me there. But it all started on a walk out to the mailbox in my SDU t-shirt...

I couldn't stop wondering why my junior season had been such a disappointment. Despite my game against Kingston, the rest of that year was a nightmare. Our team was outmatched in the next game against Liberty.

It was two days after our loss to Liberty and I was feeling sort of down. I was lying on our living room couch, flipping through the channels. I had desperately wanted to be selected for the Connie Mack League or the Area Code games. At each game, the stands are filled with college coaches and professional scouts. All the top players in Southern California compete in these summer leagues. But when the calls were made, my phone never rang. I was forced to play another summer of American Legion ball.

I sat up sharply, shut off the television, and rose to my feet. I called out to anyone who would listen. "Has anyone gotten the mail yet?" I screamed this a few times across the house, but no one answered.

I opened the front door. I was wearing a blue SDU shirt and a hat to match. I opened our mailbox and pulled out a pile of envelopes. I was very interested in the mail lately. Orlando told me he was getting letters from colleges about playing baseball. Each time I'd gone to my mailbox, I returned empty-handed. Some school in America must have at least *heard* of Jimmy Hanks.

I routinely flipped through the envelopes and magazines. A bill for mom, *Surfer Magazine* for Dave and me, a few bills for Dad, a letter for our family, another couple of bills, a letter for me from SDU, another bill for Dad. Wait, a letter for me from SDU?

I stopped, pulling the envelope from the stack. There was a big SDU emblem in the upper left-hand corner. Below it were the words, "San Diego University Athletic Department."

I ran back into the house, tripping over my sweatpants. I dropped the mail onto the counter and stared at the letter. Finally, I opened it. There was a short note inside. I read it aloud.

"Dear Jimmy:

The San Diego University baseball coaches have taken notice of your high school accomplishments. Your baseball skills could earn you a spot on the SDU baseball team. Our program looks forward to following your progress in the upcoming summer and into next season. Enclosed is an information card that will help us keep in contact with you. Please fill out this card and send it back to us as soon as possible. We wish you the best of luck in the future.

Larry Diaz
Assistant Coach
SDU Baseball

SDU had taken notice of me. I thought Larry Diaz wanted nothing to do with me. Now I'd received a letter from the greatest college baseball program in the country. This was the first time a college had noticed me. And the letter was from the only school I wanted to attend. Although this wasn't a scholarship offer, it was a good first step.

In San Diego, you're either an SDU family or a Pacific College family. We were always SDU. My two uncles went to SDU and my grandfather did as well. I didn't care how ordinary that letter was—I was going to play baseball at San Diego University.

I filled out the information card and drove down to the post office. Suddenly, my baseball career was back on track. I knew I needed a big senior year to keep SDU interested. Before the season began, I had to clear my brain. So I headed down to the basketball courts for a pick-up game. Last season, I had gotten caught up in the recruiting process. My play on the field had suffered because of it. This season, I wouldn't let that happen.

I missed the first three shots that I took and decided to move in a few steps. I dribbled toward the hoop and fired a jumper off the front of the rim. The ball shot over my head and behind me. I turned around to get the rebound. When I looked up, I saw Roger Davie, the "umbrella man."

"Mr. Davie? What are you doing here?" He collected my rebound and was holding the ball against his hip. I shook his hand, confused.

"I just went by your house. Your mom told me you were here. I always carry some hoops clothes in my trunk." He'd turned in his umbrella for a pair of basketball shorts, high-tops, and a knee brace. He bounced the ball in between his legs. "You ready?"

"Ready for what, Mr. Davie?" I was puzzled.

"Call me Roger."

"OK, Roger. What should I be ready for?"

"Getting your butt kicked." He spun the ball on his finger and laughed. "I hear you're a heck of a basketball player. But I can play a little ball myself."

"Are you serious? You want to play me?" Now I was laughing.

He fired the ball at my chest. "Check it up." He *was* serious. A professional baseball scout wanted to play me in basketball? I couldn't believe this.

"To eleven, by ones, win by two," I was speaking basketball lingo.

"All right," I checked the ball and began dribbling toward him. I faked to my left. Roger lunged for the steal and I blew right by him for an easy lay-up.

"What happened there?" I jokingly asked Roger.

"Shut up. That won't happen again." He was embarrassed, but that didn't keep him from smiling.

"One-zero, me." Again, I dribbled toward him. He retreated onto his back foot. That was all the separation I needed. Roger tried to regain his balance and put a hand in my face. I calmly drained a fourteen-foot jump shot over him. Two-nothing.

"What's up now, Roger?" I was starting to have fun. I didn't think some friendly trash talk would hurt.

"You should remember that I'm a scout for Seattle. A team that *was* thinking of picking you in the draft." Roger started laughing.

The rest of the game continued in much of the same fashion. The final score was 11-1. Roger was a good sport. "You whipped me, kid," he said as we began walking back to my house.

We walked up a steep hill as cars passed by us. "Why did you want to play me in basketball anyway?" I asked him.

"I wanted to see what kind of athlete you are," he replied.

"And?" I asked.

"You're an athlete," Roger said as he wiped the sweat from his forehead.

When the two of us got back to my house, Mom made us lemonade. We sat on the couch and talked like old pals. We spoke about baseball and wondered who would win it all this year. I mentioned to him that I wanted to go to SDU and he gave his approval.

That afternoon, Roger convinced me that my Major League dream could come true. "It will be the hardest thing you ever have to do. I see something in you, though. There's a lot of talent in that body. It's just waiting to be let out. It can happen for you if you keep working," he told me. Roger believed in me. I would never forget that. On that day, I dedicated myself to becoming a Major League baseball player.

Chapter 6: Blaine Field

The key to getting recruited is simple: be at the right place at the right time—and go three for four with a homer. Coach Edmonds always laughed when he told me this, but he was right. When the scouts are watching, you have to play well. During my senior season, I finally put everything together. I played the best baseball of my young life. But still, no college coaches called. My .444 batting average was the highest on our team and third highest in the county. But SDU hadn't contacted me since that letter arrived a year ago. I wondered if they'd forgotten about me.

Early that spring, I received news that my 3.5 grade point average had earned me an acceptance letter to SDU. I would have a chance to study finance at one of the best business schools in the country. I had my ticket to be a Shark, but not as a baseball player.

At the end of my senior year I wondered if playing college baseball team was even a possibility. That summer I decided to focus my attention on fine-tuning my baseball skills. I had made up my mind that wherever I went to school, I would try and walk on their baseball team. Just because nobody wanted to give me a scholarship didn't mean I was giving up. I knew I had to get bigger and stronger to compete at the next level. That was exactly what I did. For the first time in my life, I began lifting weights. I put on ten pounds of muscle. My six-foot frame was now two hundred pounds. I was in the best shape of my life and I was powerful.

SDU told me there was no more scholarship money left. They said I was welcome to try and walk onto the team. Translation: The SDU baseball program did not think I was good enough to be a Shark. But my summer league Coach, Dave Morris, did convince Larry Diaz to watch me play.

That final game would take place on North Beach's Blaine Field. Blaine Field was an enormous ballpark. There were a few theories about the field. People said that the thick ocean air kept baseballs in the yard. Others claimed that the size of the park was actually bigger than the numbers written on the fences. Coach Morris told us to try and hit line drives. A fly ball at Blaine Field had no chance of leaving the ballpark.

The game was about to start and I had knots in my stomach. I knew this could be my last baseball game ever. If we were eliminated and no colleges called, I would have no choice but to hang up my cleats. The next time I was at a baseball game, it could be as a spectator.

When we came back to the dugout for our first "licks," I noticed Larry Diaz behind the backstop. He was using his radar gun to clock our opponent's pitcher. "Big Boned" Lionel Strone threw real hard, over ninety miles per hour. I watched him carefully. I was starting to understand the game better and I noticed something when our leadoff hitter swung and missed on a 3–2 curve ball. Whenever Strone threw anything besides a fastball, he would fiddle with the ball in his glove. When he was going to throw heat, he would simply wind up and deliver. Strone was giving away every one of his pitches. I told the guys on the bench about this before I left the dugout for the on-deck circle.

There were runners on first and second when I came to bat. I had Strone figured out. On the first pitch, he didn't play with the ball in his glove. I knew what was coming, a fastball. That didn't matter much though. The pitch came so far inside that I nearly lost an eye. I jumped backwards and fell to the floor.

The second pitch was a real good curve. I swung and missed. I glanced back at Larry Diaz. I knew I looked bad there. The next pitch was a fastball, I could tell because Strone didn't hesitate. This one looked like a strike, too. I was ready and waiting. Instead of taking my usual stride forward, I did something different. When I saw this pitch, I reached back for more. I shifted the entire weight of my body onto my back foot. I brought my bat farther back and gathered all of my power. The next thing I heard was the "ping" of the aluminum bat.

I remember hearing Rick Ciccione's deep voice from our bench as soon as I made contact, "Oh man." He sounded like he'd seen a car accident or something.

I ran as hard as I could down the first base line. I hoped the ball would have enough juice to be out of the center fielder's reach. I was thinking double all the way.

The ball climbed higher and higher into the sky. Right as I touched first, I realized this blast wasn't coming back. I slowed my pace and stopped racing.

The ball landed well over the 400-foot sign in center field. Everyone said it couldn't be done. But I did it. I hit a home run at Blaine Field!

The crowd wasn't necessarily loud after my hit. They were more stunned. I rounded third base. Most of the fans were standing. Coach Morris's eyes were as wide as if he'd seen a ghost. He slapped me on the back as I ran past him.

Unless Larry Diaz made a trip to the bathroom, I had SDU's attention once again. I leaned back and smiled. This was my moment. Larry Diaz had now seen me play two games and I had three home runs.

I walked out to play shortstop in the bottom half of the first inning. I looked behind the backstop and noticed that Larry Diaz was not there. Had he missed my homer? I scanned the stands until I found his SDU hat. Strangely, he was next to my parents. And he wasn't the only one. There were three other scouts crowding them.

At the start of this game, nobody was interested in me. By the car ride home, my parents were telling me to expect some phone calls. Three college coaches had witnessed my blast at Blaine.

I stayed close to the phone every moment I was in the house. Two days later, it finally rang. "Hello," I said as I rolled over on my bed.

"Hello, is this Jimmy?" The voice sounded very official. I hoped that SDU had come calling.

"This is Jimmy," I said excitedly. I stood up from my bed and started walking in circles.

"Jimmy, this is George Horn. I'm the assistant baseball coach at Pacific College. It's nice to get a chance to speak with you." George who?

"It's nice to talk with you too, sir." I wasn't sure how to react to this phone call. I followed Coach Horn's lead.

"Well, I'm calling you because I'm impressed with your skills. That homer at Blaine Field was unbelievable. I've also seen your high school statistics. It seems like you're a player who has come into his own recently." He paused for a moment and then continued on. "You slipped through the cracks. And I'm one of the people who missed you. But it's not too late. Word is, you haven't decided which college you'll be attending in the fall. Is that true?" I started to feel like someone was recruiting me.

"That is true. I still don't know where I'm going. I really want to play baseball in college. I've been thinking of trying to walk on at—" I stopped before mentioning SDU. "I was going to try and walk on."

"Pacific always holds one scholarship a year for a special case, a late bloomer. This year, you're our special case. If you're interested, we'd like to offer you a scholarship to come and play baseball for us."

After everything, Pacific had offered me a scholarship. I couldn't believe it. I thanked Coach Horn, but wasn't sure what to do. Coach Horn insisted that I didn't rush my decision. He gave me his phone number and told me to give him a call. I was excited about the possibility of playing ball and attending Pacific.

So that was that. My home run at Blaine Field changed my life. Now I had a full scholarship offer from one of the top baseball programs in the country. I hung up the phone with Coach Horn and sunk back into my bed. A sense of relief came over me.

Despite the offer from Pacific, I still wanted to go to SDU. But I had to accept the fact that they hadn't contacted me. I wanted to be a Shark, but they didn't want me. I decided I would call Coach Horn and accept the scholarship. I was going to play baseball at Pacific.

Two days after my homer at Blaine, I was going through my SDU stuff to see what needed to be thrown out. I never thought this day would come. I went through a bunch of old t-shirts, some hats, a windbreaker, and the old letter from Larry Diaz. I looked at the walls of my room. I would have to replace all the SDU posters. The royal blue and white would give way to the orange and green of the Pacific Dolphins.

The next day, just before I was about to call Coach Horn, the phone rang again. This time, it was Coach Diaz. He apologized for taking so long to contact me. He had also witnessed my long home run. He confessed to me that he had always been impressed with my game. He then assured me there would be a spot for me on the SDU baseball team. But he didn't offer a scholarship. While Pacific kept one scholarship for late bloomers, SDU did not. I told him that I would need a day or two to think about what I wanted to do.

The next morning, I took a drive to the SDU campus. A half-hour after I left my house, I was standing alone on the SDU field. I took a long walk around silent Freedom Field. I thought about wearing those colors, and what that would mean to my family and me. After about fifteen minutes of thinking, I knew what I had to do. I had a chance to play baseball for the Sharks. I would never be able to forgive myself if I didn't take full advantage of it.

As soon as I got home, I found Coach Horn's phone number. "Horn," he said as he picked up the phone.

"Hi Coach, this is Jimmy Hanks."

"Hey Jimmy," he spoke excitedly.

I got right to it. "Coach, I've reached my decision. I'm sorry, but I'm going to SDU after all. Thank you for the offer, but I think this is the right decision for me."

"That's too bad. I wish you the best luck in the future, son. Maybe I'll see you in Topeka someday." Topeka, Kansas, was the site of the College Championship Series.

I smiled. "Yeah, I'll be there."

After I hung up the phone, I called Larry Diaz. I let him know that I'd be at the first practice when school started.

My Blaine Field home run had opened the doors of SDU baseball, and I walked right through them. On September 1, I arrived at San Diego University. I was a college freshman and a student athlete.

Chapter 7: Digging a Hole

I'd taken a long and bumpy road to SDU. When I finally stepped onto Freedom Field in my Sharks practice jersey, I sighed with relief. I remember the first day of practice clearly. Our team was stacked with great players—these guys were hitting bombs! And they threw harder than I'd ever seen. Their fielding was awesome. One All-American after another took batting practice. I stood with my mouth open, wondering if I was in over my head.

I stretched out by third base, getting ready for my chance to hit. Seth Ennis, an eventual starting pitcher for Pittsburgh, threw next to me. His stuff was nasty. Could I hit those pitches? Another future Major Leaguer, Jeff Jenson, smashed one fifty feet over the center field wall. Could I hit the ball that far?

Throughout that year, I played behind Ben Sutton. Ben was a freshman too, and an All-American. He was given a full scholarship. The plan was for Ben to take over as the starter when Jose Alvara graduated. So, Jose was the third baseman of the present and Ben was the third baseman of the future. And I was the other guy. I kept the faith that someday I would be the Sharks starting third baseman.

Although I didn't play much, when Coach did put me in I played well. Everything was going okay until a month into the season. The team was scheduled to go to Hawaii to play in a tournament. Only twenty-two players would be going. I figured I would be one of the lucky ones.

On the day Coach Jessup posted the list, I got up early. I threw on a pair of sweats and headed down to Freedom Field. When I got there I jumped the short fence on the third base side easily. Then I sprinted to the dugout, struggling to catch my breath.

The dugout led into our locker room. The clubhouse was silent. I opened the heavy door to Coach's office. There was a white piece of paper pinned onto his bulletin board. I went over to get a closer look. Using my finger as a marker, I worked my way down the list until I got to Henson. Wait, Henson should be after Hanks, I thought. But there *was* no Hanks. My heart sank. I hadn't made the traveling team.

I left Coach's office and went into the locker room. As I sat on the cold bench, everything came crashing down on me. I'd given up a full scholarship at Pacific to be a third stringer at SDU. I'd slipped through the cracks again.

Practice was at 3:00 p.m. the next day. I entered Coach Jessup's office at 2:15. When he saw me come in he took off his round-rimmed glasses. Coach always taught us to look people in the eye. More importantly, he taught us to have passion. I was about to show him my passion for baseball.

"What can I do for you, Jimmy?" he asked.

I was nervous. Coach Jessup only stood about

six feet tall, but his presence was larger than life. He intimidated me. "Coach, I wanted to talk to you. The past two days," I spoke meekly.

"Speak up, Jimmy," Coach was stern.

I tried to be more forceful. "I can play baseball, Coach. I believe in my abilities. What I'm trying to say is that, well, not making the traveling team really hurt. And the thing is—"

"Jimmy," Coach wasn't going to hear me out. He continued. "I also think you're a good player. I have no doubt that you're going to have a bright future. We just happen to be loaded with talent on the left side. It's not easy to find a spot for you. Over time, that'll work out. Right now, I don't have enough spots on the field for all of you." This was not what I came to hear. "But, I do believe you deserve to be making the trip to Hawaii. After I put up the roster, I added you and Craig Menson to the new list." Now *that* was what I came to hear.

I could feel my face turning bright red. I was stunned, a little embarrassed, but mostly just excited. I jumped out of my seat and shook Coach's hand. "Thank you, Coach. Thank you so much."

"You're welcome," he smiled. "Anything else?"

"No. Um ... Aloha."

In the first game against Hawaii State, Jose Alvara opened at shortstop and Ben Sutton started at third. My only chance at any action would be as a pinch hitter late in the game. But in the second inning,

Ben Sutton was hit by an inside fastball. He had to leave the game for x-rays. Ryan Gilbert came in to replace him. I got more comfy in my seat. I wouldn't be moving any time soon. Or so I thought. In the fifth inning, Jose Alvara began clutching his hamstring. I could hear his howling from the dugout. There was no doubt that his day was over. Two starters on the left side of our infield had been injured.

Coach Jessup looked down the dugout. We made eye contact. "Jimmy, get warmed up, you're in for Alvara." I tied my shoelaces and ran onto the field.

No balls were hit to me in the fifth or sixth innings. In the seventh, I belted a slider to left field for my first college homer. After I added a single in the ninth, my imagination started running wild. Maybe I *would* have a chance to be a starter this season. Thinking about the future, I lost focus on the present.

In the second game of the double-header, I started at shortstop. This was my first start in college. Everything seemed routine until the bottom half of the fourth. With a runner on first in a tie game, a laser was hit right at me. On contact, I began thinking, "Double play." I bent down to snag the grounder and flip it toward second. But the ball shot up and hit me in the chest. My error allowed no time for a throw. Instead of two outs and nobody on, there were no outs with two guys on.

I wanted another chance. I had to redeem myself. On the very next pitch, I got that chance. A soft roller was tapped my way. I had to hurry if I was going to get the runner at first. When I bent over to pick up the trickling grounder, I missed it. The ball scooted past me into left field. The lead runner scored from second. I punched my mitt. "Come on Jimmy, stay focused."

I tried to concentrate on the next batter, but my eyes were wandering. Coach Jessup was pacing in our dugout. Rudy Flowers walked the next batter on four straight pitches. The bases were now loaded. We were down by one. Coach motioned for the infield to play in on the grass. I moved in but my confidence was gone. Strikeout, bunt, hit a fly ball—just don't hit it to me.

Sure enough, the Hawaii State batter hit a 2-1 up the middle. It was a high chopper. Even in my state of mind, I knew this was an easy play. I fielded the ball cleanly and made the throw home. State's speedy Mike Stein sprinted toward the plate. My bullet beat him by at least a step. The problem was, the ball flew five feet over our catcher's head. It hit the backstop on a fly. All the runners were safe. Once again, it was my fault.

We'd fallen behind by two runs. And it was my fault. I had never been so embarrassed. I felt like digging a hole in the ground at shortstop so I could hide myself. The truth was, my three errors had already dug a hole for me.

The State fans hooted and hollered. "Shortstop,

you're terrible! We should put you in a Hawaii State jersey. You're our best player." There was nothing I could do but stand there and take it. I glanced into our dugout. Coach Jessup kicked a bunch of bats that were leaned against the wall. I'd never seen him so upset. Before the trip I told Coach Jessup that I wouldn't let him down. My actions had spoken louder than my words. I hadn't made good on my promise.

Fortunately, Rudy was able to strike out the next batter. We finally recorded our second out. I could see the escape in front of me. I desperately wanted to get out of the spotlight.

The next batter swung at an outside fastball. He barely caught the top of the pitch. Once again, the ball was hit to me. I was scared out of my mind. I shuffled to the left and put my glove down just low enough to mishandle the grounder. The ball ricocheted off my leather into left. My fourth error of the inning! This had to be a record. Two runs scored on that play and Hawaii State went ahead by four.

Coach Jessup had seen enough and pulled me from the game. Pitchers were supposed to be changed in the middle of innings, not shortstops. But I was so bad that I left Coach with no other option.

I jogged off the field. The opposing fans clapped sarcastically. Coach glared at me from the top step of the dugout. His patience was wearing thin.

Chapter 8: The Wrong Side of the Fence

As the playoffs neared, our team was on a roll. But I had little to do with the success. Coach did put me in the field for the last few innings of some games, and I only made one more error during my freshman year. That helped me earn back a reputation as a solid fielder.

Still, I suffered through a long season. Only twenty-two players traveled to conference games. Every week when the roster was posted, there was no "Hanks" on the list. So while the team made road trips all over the country, I was left alone. Usually, I would go home for the weekend. I liked being home, but my heart was someplace else. I wanted to be on the road, I wanted to be one of the guys.

The Monday practice after a road trip was always the worst for me. The guys would laugh about some funny story that happened during the weekend. I would sit there and listen. They would talk about the game and I had nothing to add. I didn't feel like a part of the team. Week after week, my insides were torn apart. I was a practice player. Sure, I would put on a uniform for home games. Maybe I'd even play an inning or two. Mostly, though, I would just sit on the bench.

At least the team was playing great. Our first-place finish in the South Pacific Conference assured us of a playoff spot. The fact that we were winning kept me motivated to work my way onto the postseason roster. If I could do that, I would have a chance to reach the College Championship Series.

The College Championship Series is played in Topeka, Kansas, every June. Most teams never reach America's heartland. Coming into my freshman year, SDU hadn't been to the Championship Series in twelve years. This team was different, though. Everyone thought we had a chance to get to Topeka. For me, I was sure this opportunity wouldn't come twice. I had to get on that playoff roster. So I kept working hard and my average crept up to around .270 for the season.

I was making progress. I was sure my progress would earn me a roster spot. In the playoffs, three additional players were added as backups. This would definitely help my chances. Who else would Coach take? I was Ben Sutton's backup. Ben's wrist had been bothering him all year long. In all likelihood, he wouldn't be able to play in the playoffs. I would have to take his place.

We finished the regular season with a record of 46-14. The day after our last game, we would leave San Diego on our road to Topeka. First, we would have to survive a four-team regional playoff to earn an invitation. Coach told us he would have the twenty-five man playoff roster on Tuesday. I'd gotten used to that white piece of paper that never had the name "Hanks" on it. With three extra spots, though, I hoped this Tuesday would be different.

Practice ended. Before long, Coach called us together for a meeting. We all took a knee and circled around him in left field. Most of us were still huffing and puffing from the sprints that ended practice. Coach was dead serious. "While you guys catch your breath, I want to congratulate you on a great regular season. I'm proud of the heart each of you has shown." Everyone smiled—except for me. I stared at Coach. I was looking for clues as to who was going to the playoffs and who was going home. He continued. "If we can show that kind of heart in the playoffs, I believe we'll be this year's National Champions."

The guys started grumbling. Coach cut us off. "First, we have to reach Topeka. And as many of you guys know, that's the toughest part." His voice got louder. "On Friday the team bus will leave here at 2:00 p.m. sharp for Sacramento and the West regional." We all started clapping. I did the same. I bumped knuckles with a few guys. I was genuinely excited. It was then that I realized something. I *was* a part of this team.

Coach Jessup momentarily lost control of his meeting. He quickly brought us back to reality. "Enough. Let's celebrate when we win the whole thing." He spoke powerfully. "I have an announcement to make about the roster for the playoffs." Everyone became silent. My heart skipped a beat. Coach cleared his throat and continued, "I'm going to use the same roster for Sacramento and Topeka. I've decided to go with the twenty-two we've traveled with all season. You guys know who you are."

That group did not include me, but I still had a chance. What about the other three spots? "I'm going with one extra catcher, and two pitchers for the three open spots. I spoke to the three of you and you also know who you are." I'd been cut again. He went on for a minute about the two pitchers and the catcher. He said they would be of the most use in case of injuries. We had enough backups in terms of position players. He apologized to everyone who wasn't making the trip. I was devastated.

The team would practice on Wednesday and Thursday. And on Friday, they would go. The guys who were not on the twenty-five-man roster were free for the summer. I struggled to fight back my tears. I came to SDU to play baseball. I didn't want to go home while my teammates played on. I wanted to tell Coach Jessup that. So I yelled out to him as he passed the pitcher's mound. "Coach," I said loudly. He turned his head and walked back toward me.

He put his arm over my shoulder. "Jimmy?"

I wasn't sure why I'd called out to him, but I knew I had to say something. "Um, I was wondering if I could continue to practice with the team. I know it's only two days, but I'd like to."

Coach patted me on the back, "Sounds good. I'll see you at practice tomorrow. And don't worry, Hanks, you're only a freshman. You've got three more shots at this."

Practice was torture during the next two days. And at 2:00 on Friday the bus to Sacramento pulled up to Freedom Field. I stood by the team that afternoon and said goodbye. I shook hands with every player and coach headed to regionals. I wished them luck and told them I believed they would win the whole thing.

The bus slowly moved out of the parking lot. I watched it for as long as I could. I'm not sure what I was hoping for. Maybe the bus would turn around and Coach would ask me to come along. No such luck. Twenty-five of my teammates and best friends pulled away in search of their dreams. A few minutes later, I pulled away in search of my lost baseball career.

I settled in at home. I got out my surfboard and started my vacation. Mom and Dad were proud because I had earned a perfect 4.0 in school that semester. I was happy too. My good grades gave me career options beyond baseball. Still, I couldn't stop thinking about the team. I followed them every step of the way on the internet and in the papers. They were rolling through regionals. With each victory, they moved closer to Topeka.

The morning after the final game in Sacramento,

I jumped out of bed, ran down the steps and out the front door. I opened the newspaper and threw everything but the sports page to the concrete. The headline read, "At Last! Sharks Headed Back to Topeka!" The guys had done it. They were going to Topeka!

Later that night, I thought about my missed opportunity. The team was going to Topeka and I was going to dinner. I was silent at the table. I stared into my food. Then my mother said the strangest thing to me. "Jimmy?"

"Yeah, Mom?" I looked away from my mashed potatoes.

"Do you want to drive to Topeka?" Mom asked.

"What are you talking about?" I said, wondering if I was hearing things.

"Do you want to drive to Topeka? You and me."

I looked over at Dad. He shrugged his shoulders and smiled. Obviously he was in on this plan as well. "Drive to Topeka? Are you crazy?" I thought they were both losing their minds. Maybe they'd overdosed on broccoli or something.

"I'm serious, let's go. It'll be fun." Mom started to laugh a little. I raked my fork through my mashed potatoes. I shaped them into a baseball diamond. I thought about her suggestion. Drive to Topeka, see the guys, and go to the College Championship Series. My mind was made up. "If you're serious, I'm in."

After dinner that night, we mapped out our trip and packed our stuff into Mom's Jeep. We left early the next morning for a three-day drive to Topeka. We would be arriving the night before our first game. Mom saved the day.

A few days later, we entered the ballpark around 8:45 a.m. I walked around the stadium so I could see the names of all the Major Leaguers who'd played in Topeka. Rockport Stadium had hosted some amazing games. I made my way down the steps to the edge of the SDU dugout. I watched the guys talk to one another, toss the baseball, and chew on seeds. Finally, I caught the eye of Jose Alvara.

"Hey," I shouted to him in the dugout.

Jose looked at me and pointed, "Hanks!" Suddenly the entire bench exploded. The guys started running over to see if it was really me. Everyone was great. They thanked me for coming all the way to Topeka to support them. It was one of the great moments of my life. For those ten minutes, I was a part of the team again—even though I was on the wrong side of the fence.

Coach Jessup was the last one to come over and say hello. "You got heart, kid. If you want to come sit on the bench with your teammates, you're more than welcome."

The guys made me feel welcome, even though I was wearing street clothes. I sat in my blue jeans and my SDU hat. I cheered loudly as they advanced to the final game of the College Championship Series. But during those five games, I did not step between the lines of Rockport Field. I wasn't there as a player. I didn't belong on that field.

The championship game was against our biggest rival, Pacific. This was the same school that had offered me a scholarship last season. The players took batting practice and I walked around the back of the cage. I watched the teams get ready for the biggest game of their lives.

Most of the players from SDU and Pacific knew each other. These guys pretty much all grew up playing ball in Southern California. I moved around the cage, but made sure never to touch fair territory.

From behind the batter's box I recognized an old friend of mine. It was Pacific's assistant coach, George Horn. The same Coach Horn who'd watched me play at Blaine Field a year earlier. I walked over to him. The "pinging" of the aluminum bats was a loud background noise. "Coach Horn," I called out to him.

He looked in my direction. "Jimmy Hanks, how are you?"

The last time I talked to him was when I had decided to go to SDU instead of Pacific. "I could be better." I pointed to my outfit. This made him aware that I had not been asked to wear a uniform to the game. "I'm not complaining, just happy to be here."

"How'd your season go?" He asked.

"Some ups and some downs. A few hits, a few

errors. I'm hoping that I get a chance to be a starter next year." I really thought that this was a possibility.

"You'll get your chance. Be patient, you're a good ballplayer."

"Thanks, Coach."

I couldn't help but wonder what would have happened if I went to Pacific instead of SDU. If I would have said "yes" to Coach Horn that day on the phone, things might have been different. I might have been wearing a uniform that afternoon instead of a windbreaker.

We said goodbye and Coach Horn wished me luck. I made my way down the third base line. I looked at the chalk that separated the playing field from foul territory. My teammate, Brendan Hershey, came up from behind me. He tossed me a mitt. "Hey, Jimmy, you want to have a catch?"

I looked at the chalked lines again. "Nah, I'm fine. I'm going to stay over here, you know." I wasn't going to step onto that field. Brendan nodded his head. He understood.

The freshly cut grass and the evenly raked in-field dirt looked perfect. I made a pact with myself. I would do everything in my power to get back to Topeka, as a player. Then I could walk onto this field with my head high and a Sharks uniform on my back.

The final score that day was 11-5. Pacific College dominated us from the get-go. They were crowned 1995 Champions. Before I left the stadium, I threw some dirt from behind the batting cage into my pocket. I wanted to take a small piece of Rockport Field with me. When I got home, I put that piece of Topeka into a small envelope. One day, I hoped to return that dirt to the field I took it from.

Chapter 9: It's Just a Game

My memory continued to run wild. My life was playing in front of me like a movie. And all the while, I was fighting to survive. But I could feel myself beginning to lose energy. I was underwater. I was blind. I didn't know which way was up or which way was down. I was out of breath. It had been a while since that last wave had hit.

These thoughts put me into a panic. My legs began to kick and my arms pumped hard as well. There was no way I was going to give up on life. I had too much to fight for. I desperately needed some air. And I needed it right away...

The time was now. This was all I could think about when I arrived at SDU for my sophomore season. I had a fresh start ahead of me and was determined to make my career a success. I began lifting weights again and running long distances every afternoon.

In the off-season, Ben Sutton had signed a contract with San Diego and Jose Alvara had graduated. This left Gilbert, Cilla, and me as the three guys on the left side of the infield. I knew Ryan Gilbert was probably going to be the starting shortstop. And although Ernie Cilla was a good ballplayer, I was sure third base would be my position.

About five weeks before our first practice, I

had a talk with Ryan that turned my plans upside down. We sat next to each other in accounting class. We were friends, though we only talked about baseball. We started to chat about the upcoming season. I told him that I thought he'd be our starting shortstop, and that I'd start at third.

He quickly ended my dreams. "I guess you didn't hear, huh?"

"Hear what?" Our professor arrived and Ryan looked straight ahead.

I had to know what he was talking about. "What? Hear what, Ryan?" I whispered.

He whispered back. "We signed a shortstop yesterday."

Oh no, I thought. He continued, "A freshman All-American two years ago. Desmond Samuel, a transfer from Trenton College. You ever heard of him?"

I had heard of him. He was a great ballplayer. Part of me was excited because our team was getting another excellent player. But another part of me was crushed. I was staring another season of bench-warming right in the face. Samuel would be our starting shortstop. This meant that Ernie, Ryan and I would compete for playing time at third base. Nothing at SDU was coming easy for me.

I showed up for practice on January 2nd. Upon my arrival, the dogfight for third began. Luckily, I was playing the best baseball of my entire life. My line drives were bullets. I was hitting to all fields with power.

I had no idea what was happening. Something clicked, I guess.

Two days before our first game, Ernie Cilla was eliminated from the competition for the starting spot. He was hit by a tailing fastball that broke his arm in two places. I felt terrible for Ernie. I also knew that his injury meant either Ryan or I would be the Sharks starting third baseman.

When our first game against Upper Nevada finally arrived, I was excited. I was sure I would be seeing my name in the starting lineup. But when I checked the card, I received the same old news. Ryan Gilbert was penciled in as the starting third baseman. I started my sophomore season in a familiar seat, on the bench. What would I have to do to earn Coach Jessup's respect? I sat through the entire first game wondering.

The game was close and Coach began to pace around the dugout. He noticed me moping at the end of the bench. He sensed my frustration. "Hanks, get over here," he yelled. Seth Ennis moved away from Coach. This left an open seat next to him. I sat down. He didn't look happy with me. "I want you to stop your pouting. You're not helping this team by sitting in the dugout with a long face. This is supposed to be fun. Now grab a helmet, you're pinch hitting."

I came to the plate in the seventh inning excited for my at bat. To my surprise, a familiar face was there to greet me on the pitcher's mound. Josh Green had played his high school baseball in San Diego. I'd faced him a bunch of times. This eased my nerves when I dug in for the first at bat of my sophomore season.

Coach had given me a chance. I had to do something to prove that I deserved to be on that field. After working the count full, I swung at a change-up and connected. The ball cleared the right field fence easily. The pitch had hit the fat part of my bat and my legs lifted it out of the park. I wanted to pump my fists, but I didn't. I tried to act like I'd been in this situation before.

That hit changed everything for me. I started every game for the rest of my career as a Shark. Soon enough I was getting hits every day. Pete Jacquez and Jeff Engle, both current Major Leaguers, hit third and fourth. And *I* hit fifth. I was the sophomore with no scholarship! I was the guy who no one believed in. I was hitting fifth and helping one of the best teams in America win ballgame after ballgame.

My sophomore year went great. I batted .342 with ten home runs. I helped us win the conference for the second straight year. Of course, this success got me dreaming big again, and I was dreaming of Topeka. But those dreams all crashed when Cheyenne beat us in the regional.

Individually, I was pleased with my sophomore season. I began to think about entering the Major League Draft after my junior year. Up until that year, my after-college plans did not include baseball. I was sure I would simply move back to Oceantown and become a banker. I'd done everything that was necessary to achieve that goal. But after my sophomore season, banking was the last thing on my mind.

We were only two days away from the first game of my junior season. Before the madness began, I had a few minutes to relax. I was lying down in my apartment when a phone call jerked me out of bed.

"Jimmy?" the voice on the other end asked.

"Yeah," I said in a tired groan.

"You know who this is?"

I knew exactly who it was. That same voice had once convinced me that I was a baseball ballplayer. "Of course I do, O." It was Orlando. I hadn't heard from him in about two months. The first few minutes of that conversation was mostly small talk. We did the regular stuff people do when they haven't spoken in a while. When we'd finished telling our stories Orlando offered me some other news. "Before I hang up, I was saving some great news for you." I could tell he was smiling on the other end.

"What news?" I asked excitedly.

"I was talking to this Milwaukee scout yesterday. He asked me if I still kept in contact with you. Anyway, he starts rambling about how he used to scout California. He saw us both play in high school. Then he says—now get this—he and his scouts have you projected as a first through fourth round pick in the draft. First through fourth! That's big time, bro. I thought that you—"

I cut Orlando off. "First through fourth! He really said that?"

"First through fourth." He repeated.

I took a moment to collect my breath. I struggled to find words to keep a conversation going. I was too busy replaying the words "first through fourth" over and over again in my head.

Orlando had one last comment before he hung up. It was the same comment he constantly reminded me of. "Aren't you glad I told you baseball was your sport? You could be on some basketball court right now, waiting for a pick-up game." He laughed loudly.

"I'm glad I listened to you. Thanks O." The conversation was over and I hung up the phone.

My junior season was about to start and I was a prospect. I was a player people had heard of. Scouts from twenty-five of thirty major league teams had contacted me. If I was selected high enough in June's draft, I would give up my senior year of college to play minor league baseball for a major league organization.

I approached my junior season with a new attitude. This cockiness, however, turned out to be the worst mistake I ever made in baseball. I began to put pressure on myself. The tension had me swinging for home runs like I was Babe Ruth. Instead, I was striking out like Ruth Hanks, my grandma. In trying to impress everyone, I fell flat on my face.

I kept taking extra batting practice, but that didn't seem to work. I slept with my bat, but still I couldn't hit. I started eating chicken instead of pasta before games. I even asked my brothers for help. Nothing got me out of my slump. I was hitting .198 through the first twenty games. If I had any hope of playing baseball beyond college, I knew I would have to step up my game quickly.

We'd already finished one-third of the season. Although I was still hitting fourth in the lineup, I was killing the team. Finally, some advice from an old friend rid me of my anxiety. We were ten minutes away from the first pitch in a game against Phoenix College. I sipped water from a fountain close to our dugout. It was there that I heard a familiar voice, "Hey, Hanks."

I turned around and saw Roger Davie. We hadn't seen one another in awhile. We started to talk about what was happening to me on the baseball field. Roger had noticed the decline in my numbers. He asked me what the problem was. I told him that my hands felt slow. And that I was taking my eye off the ball too.

Roger cut me off: "That's all bull and you know it. What happened to the smiling kid I knew in high school? You're too serious Hanks...bat speed, and your eyes. If you want to succeed in baseball, you have to have passion. It sounds like you're more wor-ried about being a high draft-pick than a ballplayer.

It's just a game, Jimmy. Now let me see that high school smile."

I smiled for Roger, and it was a real one. He was right. In the race to be a high draft-pick, I forgot how much I loved baseball. I loved the one-on-one showdown between the batter and the pitcher. I loved the smell of fresh oil in my glove. I loved the sound of a collision at home plate. I loved the helmet slaps and the baseball chatter in the dugout. I missed *playing* the game. I wanted to have fun again. When I shook Roger's hand, a weight lifted from my shoulders.

Ryan Gilbert saw me grinning when I came back into the dugout. "What the heck are you so happy about?" he asked.

I looked at Ryan, still smiling. "I'm back," I told him. And I was.

I did what Roger had told me. I came to the plate smiling. The result was a home run. The baseball landed forty feet beyond the fence in left. As I crossed home plate, I looked above our dugout. There was Roger. He nodded his head and I nodded back.

I ended up hitting ten home runs in the last forty games of that season. My batting average shot up over one hundred points too. My concerns were no longer affiliated with the draft. I simply wanted to win. And we did win, forty-five times to be exact. Our season ended, though, with a heartbreaking 9-8 loss to Birmingham in the playoffs.

On the plane ride home, I thought about the

goal I had set two years ago. I wasn't so sure that I would reach Topeka. I sat back and watched the plane soar through the clouds and over the Rocky Mountains. I was in my own world. I wondered, if after my junior season, my college career would be over.

Bryan Vogelsong, my best friend on the team, tapped me on the shoulder. "So is that it?" I had been asking myself the same question. I'd dreamed of wearing the royal blue and white since I was a kid. Could I give up my last year in a Shark uniform? Could I give up my last chance at Topeka?

Bryan repeated his question, "So, is that it? Are you done?"

"Is what it?" I turned to face him, buying time by repeating his question.

"Was that the last time we'll ever see Jimmy Hanks at third base for the Sharks?"

Bryan took a sip of his orange juice and looked at me. I stared off in the opposite direction, unable to answer.

Chapter 10: Getting Up

It was day two of the Major League Draft. The Hanks house was silent. Mom and Dad were at work. My brothers were out surfing. Everyone knew I needed to be alone that day. The first day of the draft had come and gone. I hadn't been selected.

On the first day, seven hundred and fifty players were chosen. Three guys on my team were drafted in the top sixteen rounds. Seth Ennis and Rudy Flowers were selected in the ninth and tenth rounds. Desmond Samuel became a fifteenth round choice for Boston. While they began to plan a future in baseball, I waited for the phone to ring.

The second morning turned into afternoon and the phone sat quietly next to me. At five o'clock I gave up. I walked over to the computer and clicked onto the Major League Baseball web site. There was a message written in large, capital letters:

THE1997 MAJOR LEAGUE DRAFT IS NOW OVER. FIFTEEN HUNDRED PLAYERS FROM HIGH SCHOOLS, JUNIOR COLLEGES, AND COLLEGES HAVE BEEN SELECTED BY THIRTY DIFFERENT FRANCHISES. MAJOR LEAGUE BASEBALL WISHES ALL OF THESE BALLPLAYERS THE BEST OF LUCK IN THEIR QUEST TO BECOME MAJOR LEAGUERS.

I tossed the phone onto the couch. Two days, fifty rounds, fifteen hundred players, and no Jimmy Hanks.

I grabbed keys to my truck and stormed outside. I had to get out of my house. I didn't want to face the curious eyes of my brothers. I couldn't handle the sad look on Mom's face. Dad would have some words of wisdom, but they wouldn't do me any good. Not in my state of mind. So I drove off.

I drove down streets that I'd driven down my entire life. Something was strange, though. Something was wrong. I didn't know where I was going anymore. I felt lost. My dreams were crumbling before my eyes.

An hour later, I ended up at Coastal Field. I didn't know what brought me there. I got out of my truck and walked down the steps towards the first base line. Right away, I knew there was no place I'd rather be. I always felt better when I stepped onto a baseball diamond. Even though it was baseball that kept breaking my heart, I still loved it. I walked around the field. I could see that baseball was in season. The smeared chalk lines had recently been stepped on. I wondered if I'd just missed a game.

I had played on this field as a kid, so I knew it pretty well. There was a bench beyond the outfield fence with the coolest view. I made my way to the deepest part of the ballpark and climbed over the short fence. I took a seat. The view was of the Pacific Ocean. There was no one in sight. I leaned back, deep in thought.

With the fading sun in the background I watched the waves crash below me. Baseball was hurting me so much. And for the first time ever, I thought about giving it up. I was sick and tired of having baseball kick my butt. I was tired of expectations that were never met. There were plenty of other things I could do. I had options because I was well-educated. I was going to receive my college degree in less than a year. I thought back to my original plan of becoming a banker. I wondered if I would ever be able to walk away from baseball. I turned this question over and over in my head.

How *could* I walk away after all I'd been through? I started to recall all the tough times. I remembered sitting in my kitchen after getting cut from the Tidal Waves. I thought about walking into Bayside High School as "the new kid." I could still see the image of Larry Diaz walking past me after my two-homer game. I heard the fans laughing in Hawaii. I remembered sitting in the dugout in Topeka. I was wearing blue jeans, while my teammates fought for a Championship.

I'd gotten up each and every time I'd been knocked down before. "I can take more punches than you can." I've lived by those words. I could never quit. I turned around and stared at the bases, the pitcher's mound and the outfield fence. I should have been fed up with baseball—striking out, making errors, and missing chances. But I wasn't. I'd just driven an hour, on the worst day of my baseball life, to a ballpark. I wanted so badly to play the game I loved for a living. I would give every ounce of myself to be a Major Leaguer. It was no longer about getting a chance—it was about making something happen.

I stood up and hopped over the fence. I was through sitting. I began walking towards the batter's box. Once I got there I asked an imaginary umpire for timeout. He granted me my wish. I adjusted my imaginary helmet as I dug in. I listened to the crowd roar at the empty field. Suddenly, I had my favorite bat on my shoulder. I was wearing a Major League uniform, and my name was on the towering scoreboard. "Now batting, the third baseman, number 30, Jimmy Hanks." I tipped my hat to the imaginary crowd. I looked up at the scoreboard. It was the World Series, game seven, two outs, bases loaded, we're down by three, bottom of the ninth. I'd been up in that situation a million times in my dreams.

I stood in the batter's box and stared down the pitcher. He spit onto the ground. I could hear my teammates rooting me on in the background. I cocked my bat and got ready. The first pitch was a curve ball that caught the outside corner for a strike. "Beat me there," I thought. I stared down at the third base coach who gave me the "swing away" sign. I was ready again.

The next pitch was straight heat just over the outside corner. I reached out for the fastball and crushed it to center field. The ball rose quickly. I leaned forward, trying to convince it to leave the park. Does it have enough? Does it have enough? The center fielder was running toward the wall, timing his jump. It's going, it's going. He leaped high in the air—but it's gone! A home run! Home run, Jimmy Hanks to win the World Series!

I trotted around the bases slowly. When I crossed home plate, I sat down. Instantly, I was all alone. The dream was over and I was back in my scrubby jeans and SDU hat. The field was once again dead silent. In the silence, I realized where I was going: back to SDU for my senior season.

I spent the next couple of days surfing with my brothers. A week later a phone call convinced me to trade in my wet suit for a uniform. Coach Tollberg wanted me to play summer ball in Cape Cod, Massachusetts. The Cape Cod League was the best summer league in the country. It was an opportunity I couldn't refuse. I packed up my stuff and boarded a flight to the Cape that night. Baseball had called, and I answered.

In Cape Cod, against the best pitching college baseball had to offer, I batted .300. Again, many scouts told me they were interested in drafting me. Again, I heard that I would be a top ten round draft pick. This time, I knew better than to listen. If I ignored the predictions, I wouldn't be upset if I wasn't drafted. My goal was to enjoy the ride of being a senior in college.

I had no idea it would turn out to be the ride of my life.

I knew that our team was going to be good that year. I just didn't know how good. Seth Ennis turned down a contract from St. Louis to make a run at the Championship. His return meant that our staff had an ace. Eli Menson, who would later reach the Majors, was our catcher. He supplied big power in the middle of our lineup. Most of the guys who I'd spent my college career with returned. We all wanted that Championship.

The 1998 Sharks had everything—pitching, defense, power, speed, and hitting. Still, I knew how many miles we'd have to travel to reach Topeka. We couldn't afford to get ahead of ourselves. If we did, my dream of returning that dirt to Rockport Stadium would be over.

The night before the season started, I took out the envelope I'd placed the dirt in. I opened it up. I put my finger inside and felt around. Tomorrow morning marked the start of my senior season—my last chance. I had to get to Topeka.

Chapter 11: The Promised Land

As the regular season ended, the focus shifted toward the playoffs. We'd won ten of our final twelve games. That exclamation point on a great regular season earned us the number one seed in the East Regional. A ticket to Topeka would be on the line in Durham, North Carolina.

In the opening game, Seth Ennis lived up to his reputation as a top college pitcher. He silenced the bats of Hamlitt University. Our lineup continued a hot month of hitting. We opened up the playoffs with a 10-3 victory. Our momentum slowed, though, when Virginia Southern pounded us, 14-4 in the next game. This loss brought back some bad memories.

One more loss and our season would be over. One more loss and my college career would be done, too. One more loss and the promise of reaching Topeka would be broken.

In order to advance from the loser's bracket, we would have to win three games on the same day. Our first assignment was the Durham Dogs. They had the advantage of playing a home game. The Dogs' fans came out in full force. But our bats made the most noise on that morning. The 8-5 victory put us in the finals against Birmingham, who hadn't lost. This meant we'd have to beat them twice in a row to advance.

We fought them off in the afternoon game with a 3-2 win. This forced one final game, winner advancing and loser going home.

The East Regional final against Birmingham was the best college baseball game I ever played in. Birmingham took an early 1-0 lead with a home run in the bottom of the first. Half an inning later we were slapping hands in our dugout after regaining the lead. Before we could catch our breath, Birmingham struck back. We were down again, 3-2.

By the time this "tug of war" reached the bottom of the ninth, we had regained the lead at 4-3. They had a runner on third base with one out against our closer, Jack Kater. The tying run was on third base, just ninety feet from home. I started thinking about extra innings. Jack had other ideas. He promptly struck out the next batter. This left us one out away from Topeka.

The next guy up was an excellent left-handed hitter. As soon as he made contact with Jack's fastball, I was sure the game would be tied. It looked as if he had found the only hole in our infield. Jack's slider was tattooed between Stan Davis and Will Russell, our middle infielders. Stan moved to his left, but had no chance to make the play. Will shuffled to his right and went airborne to preserve our lead. The bouncing ball appeared to be out of his reach. It hopped high above his head as he dove across the infield dirt. Will extended his arm farther than I could imagine. Somehow, he speared the ball over his head. In the most athletic play I'd ever seen, he jumped up and threw a strike to first. His toss beat the runner by a hair! The umpire's "out" signal ended the game and kicked off our celebration.

I ran over to Will and tackled him. The two of us became the bottom of a growing pile. Soon, we were crushed by our teammates. We didn't care though. We were headed to Topeka for the College Championship Series.

We arrived in Topeka three days after our return trip to San Diego. Our first opponent was Louisiana College and their famous "gorilla ball." This term defined their ability to hit home run after home run.

I put on my glove, fixed my hat, and stepped out of the dugout with a kick to my step. I glanced around at the television cameras, the huge stadium, and the screaming fans. I got the chills as I approached the infield dirt. I stopped and stared down at the chalked line in front of third base. I was finally going to cross the line as a player. But there was something I had to do first. I reached into my back pocket and pulled out my envelope. I bent over and emptied the dirt back onto the field. I'd made good on my promise to return the borrowed earth. I moved the dirt back and forth with my cleat, mixing the old with the new. When the brown blended together I felt as though I had accomplished something great.

I punched the center of my mitt. "Let's go Jimmy, time to play some gorilla ball."

As it turned out, "gorilla ball" was simply too much for us that day. Louisiana College lived up to their reputation and blasted seven home runs. They beat us, 11-10. Again, we'd lost our first game. We now faced the challenge of winning five games in a row against the nation's best teams. If we lost once, our dream season was over.

In the first game, we nipped the University of New York, 8-7. Orlando played for UNY, so that vic tory was sweet and sour. I was sad to end the dream of my good friend.

After that win we had a full day of rest. The next game would be versus River College the follow-ing night. My day off was also the first day of the 1998 Major League Draft—hardly a relaxing break. The memories of last year still haunted me. As the first day of selections neared its end, I hadn't been chosen. The same sick feeling I felt a year ago was back. This time, the pain was sharper. This was my last chance to get drafted.

During the second day of the draft I was twice as nervous. I sat close to the phone in my hotel room from the moment I woke up. No one called. Again, I was left asking myself questions that I had no answers to. I killed time by playing cards with my roommate, Will Russell. Will was a fellow senior who was hoping for a similar phone call.

At 12:30 p.m. we put down the cards and headed to lunch. I hoped that when we returned, the message light would be lit. An hour later, Will and I returned. The light was not flashing. So the torment continued for both of us. I began to think that I'd been overlooked once again. We would leave for the field—and the draft would be over—in an hour. Time was running out on my dreams.

I pulled up my left stirrup and got ready for what could have been the last game of my baseball career. Will was in the shower and I was alone with my thoughts. I walked over to the TV and clicked it on. Then I bent down to yank on my other stirrup. And then the phone rang. At first, I just stared at it nervously. I wanted to move, but was scared the call wasn't for me. It rang again. I grabbed the receiver.

"Hello," I shouted.

"Hey, Jimmy, this is Doug Deaver from the Dallas Lonestars." I knew who Doug was.

"Hey Doug, how's it going?" This could be the call.

"Great, it's going great. You ready for your game tonight?"

"I already have my stirrups on."

"Well, I have some good news for you. We just picked you in today's draft. Congratulations, you're a member of the Dallas Lonestars organization."

I pumped my fist in the air and tried to regain my breath. I managed to calm myself enough to speak.

"Thank you so much, Doug. I've been waiting for this phone call for a long time. You made my dream come true today. I guarantee you won't be sorry you drafted me." I paused. "I'm a Lonestar."

I couldn't believe it. I would have a chance to play Minor League Baseball after all. I felt like I'd just won the lottery. But in reality, I knew I hadn't received this call by chance. Although I wasn't always the best athlete, I was usually the hardest worker. Getting drafted was my reward.

On the bus ride over to the field, I told a few guys about my selection. I didn't want to make a big deal about it. We had to focus on the task at hand, River College. We arrived at the stadium with a sense of purpose. So did our pitcher, Ralph Held. The freshman was amazing. He struck out 14 batters and we got an easy 8-1 victory.

Now we were just three victories away from the Championship. First we'd have to beat the Louisiana College Crawfish twice in a row. If our dream was going to continue, our pitchers had to be great. They would have to find some way to keep the ball in the park.

I guess someone told that to Seth Ennis. Our ace limited the Crawfish to only three runs in our 6-3 victory in the first game. We returned to play Louisiana the next night and Mike Bender was just as dominant. He didn't back down from the Crawfish hitters. Instead, he busted his fastball in on their hands. One big bat after another barely hit weak ground balls to our infielders. An 8-3 victory put us in the championship game against Santa Fe University. One game would decide which team would be the 1998 National Champions.

Santa Fe threw their best pitcher against us, a lefty named Roy Gibbs. Roy had been the third pick in the first round of the draft a few days earlier. We congratulated him by scoring five runs in the top of the first. We then scored three more in the second to take an 8-0 lead.

The title was within our grasp. We shifted into cruise control. In the dugout, we began to count the outs until a championship. We should have been counting the seconds until Santa Fe woke up. We lost sight of our goal and Santa Fe took advantage. They scored ten runs in the next five innings.

When the game entered the top of the seventh, our lead was 13-10. We needed some insurance runs. I was the leadoff hitter in our half of the seventh. I did my job and singled to left. A few batters later, I was standing on third with two outs. The bases were loaded behind me. This was our chance to put them away. Will Russell was at the plate. He'd already pounded four hits in four at-bats. One more and he could put this one out of reach.

On the first pitch, I tried to distract Chip Williams, Santa Fe's relief pitcher. I charged down the third base line. Not only was he not distracted, he never even looked at me. He remained focused. He had Russell pinned against the wall with a 1-2 count.

Before the next pitch, I looked over at Coach Jessup in the dugout. The sun was in my eyes. I thought I saw him touch the tip of his hat and wipe his hands down his thighs. That's the steal sign. How could he be giving me the steal sign? I shrugged my shoulders. He repeated the signal. There it was again. He touched the tip of his hat and then wiped his hands down his thighs. Coach wanted me to steal home. I tipped my helmet to him and nodded. I was ready.

As soon as I got the sign, my palms started to sweat. "Get a good jump and be fast," I kept thinking to myself as I tried to find oxygen. I took a few steps off third base. The time moved in slow motion. It was just the pitcher and me. My job was to beat his pitch to the plate, ninety feet away. If I was safe, our three-run cushion would become a four-run advantage. If I was out, I would kill our rally. A mistake like that could inspire a Sante Fe comeback.

I increased my lead to about six steps off the bag. I watched the pitcher as carefully as I could. Again, he never looked in my direction. I extended my lead a few more feet. I was waiting for him to pull off the rubber and throw over to third. I was also waiting for the beginning of his windup. Either way, when he moved, I would start my sprint home.

There it was. The instant he started his windup, I was off. I put my head down and motored as fast as

I could. Williams noticed me taking off, and rushed his delivery. By the time I was halfway down the line, I was sure I was a dead duck. I neared home and looked up, angling my slide. Just as the ball arrived at the plate, so did I. I wasn't sure if I'd beaten the tag. The umpire would have the final say. My toe touched the bag and I felt the catcher's glove on my thigh. I stared up through a cloud of dust to see the umpire, "Safe! Safe! Safe!" he shouted into the Topeka sky. I had stolen home plate!

I tumbled out of my slide and started pumping my fists. When I got into the dugout, the guys were all pounding my helmet. We had a 14-10 lead and we were back in control! After the celebration, Bryan Vogelsong, "the king of stats," approached me with a surprise. "You did it, man, 20-20. The first man in Sharks history." That stolen base was my 20th of the season. I became the first Shark to ever steal twenty bases and hit twenty home runs in the same season.

Before I could catch my breath, Will stung the next pitch to right center field. His single knocked in two runs and gave us a 16-10 lead. We went on to win by a football-like tally of 21-14.

For twenty-five guys and six coaches, there was no greater sight in the world than seeing Jack Kater strike out that final batter. We mobbed the field as champions. In the middle of the pile on the pitcher's mound, I spotted Bryan Vogelsong. Now, I had a stat for him. "The 1998 San Diego University Sharks are

Champions. Put that one in your stat book, Bry, and don't ever forget it."

Chapter 12: Baseball, Without the Perks

In the middle of my underwater daydream I felt a pair of arms wrap around my chest. A moment later I felt the air hit my face. I took the deepest breath of my life. I kept breathing in and out as Orlando paddled and kicked his feet. I held onto his arms tightly. I was too shocked to open my eyes at first. By the time I did, Jen and Maria were holding me up as well, swimming me back to shore.

It turned out that I had hit my head on a rock. I got twenty-two stitches later that night. I'd nearly been knocked unconscious out there. I'd been fighting with the waves for about a minute or so, but it felt like an hour. I relived my entire life out there.

Orlando swam me back to shore and laid me down on the cool sand. I took a few more deep breaths and spit out the salty water from within my chest. "You alright, Jimmy?" Orlando asked, "Can you hear me?"

"Yeah, I hear you." I reached out and touched my hand to Orlando's shoulder.

"That was some wave, huh?" Orlando asked with a sheepish grin. He put a towel on my head to control the bleeding.

"Some wave is right," I laughed, relieved that I was on the shore. "You really saved me this time."

"You really saved me this time." Orlando said as he gathered the rest of his things together and boarded the bus. Orlando and I were roommates. And just like in high school, he never woke up on time.

"I'm buying you a new alarm clock. I've been waking your lazy butt up since sixth grade." We sat down in a seat next to one another near the back of the bus.

The engine started in the 5:00 a.m. darkness of Auburn, New York.

Orlando tapped me on the shoulder. "Hey Jimmy, can you believe this?" Orlando smiled. We were both excited for our first Minor League bus trip. Orlando was also a selection of the Lonestars in the 1998 draft. Once again, we were teammates. "Here we are, a couple of pro ballplayers. Going after the same dreams we talked about in high school. You know I was –"

I cut him off. "I know, you were the first person to tell me that I was a ballplayer."

"Well I was." Orlando smiled. He was wide awake, and got up to introduce himself to a few of the guys. I shook some hands as well. It was final. My life as a professional baseball player had begun.

I was real tired that morning. Waking up early had never been one of my favorite activities. Eight-hour bus rides starting at 5:00 a.m. sounded about as much fun as a dentist appointment. At least Orlando was there with me. He sat back down in the seat next to me. I zoned out, thinking about life at home. I thought about all the guys I knew who had just graduated. They would begin careers in law, medicine, and finance. I wondered what their first day of work would be like. This was mine.

Orlando was talking again, "I can't believe you beat me in my last college game." I laughed at his comment. He continued, "Then you win the College Championship. And three days later, the two of us are sitting on a bus at dawn. Baseball's a funny game, huh? You start playing, and soon, it means everything to you. The friends you meet along the way—they're the same guys you pass going around the bases. They're the ones sitting next to you on a bus ride to Vermont. It's awesome, you know?"

"Yeah, it really is." I felt like I was back in high school again as I listened to Orlando talk my ear off. I gave him a knuckle-bump and leaned my head against the window. I was hoping to catch up on some sleep.

In the span of three days, I had gone from College Champion to Minor League nobody. I didn't care. Someone was paying me to play baseball. My office was a baseball field. Baseball was my job. How could baseball ever be a job? I would soon find out, the hard way.

The hard way means eight-hour bus trips. It means being thousands of miles away from home. It means living out of a suitcase and learning how to sleep squeezed against the window of a bus. I learned about different cities and states that once seemed foreign to me. When I was at SDU, I was a short drive from a family dinner. Those days were over.

I had been assigned to Auburn, New York, the home of the lowest rookie ball team for the Lonestars Organization. Their were five teams I had to advance through before becoming a Major League player, and a Lonestar. I would spend this season playing in the East Coast League. I was a professional player, but I was a long way from the majors.

We made weekly road trips to New York, Massachusetts, Pennsylvania, and Vermont. Shuttling in and out of hotels and buses became a way of life. This was what Minor League Baseball *really* was, baseball without the perks.

I was having a hard time falling asleep on that first road trip. I moved around in my seat. A moment later, Coach Sam Goddfrey stood in front of the team. He officially welcomed the new guys. "Fellas, I need to make an announcement before you fall asleep." He rubbed his moustache and continued. "Today, we're welcoming some new guys to our club. If you gentlemen would stand up."

I stood along with Orlando and a few other guys. We all tipped our hats or gave a small wave. Not that anyone cared, or even looked up. In the Minor Leagues, you never like to see more players added to your team. Guys have to look out for their next paycheck. A new player means that someone else is after your roster spot. We quietly sat back down.

"I'll tell you the same thing I told the rest of these guys when they arrived. Big dreams start small, and they start now. I don't care what you did as a kid, in high school, or in college. Today is the first day of your life. One out of ten guys on this bus will put on a Major League uniform, maybe fewer than that. The chances are slim and the road is long. I know. I've been in your seat as a player, and I never made it to the 'show.' I respect you all for trying. All I ask is that you play as hard as you can every night. That's the truest test of who will survive out here and who won't."

I knew the odds were against me when I came to Auburn, but I wouldn't let that stop me.

During the next two months, I played baseball six days a week. I slept in roadside motels and ate fast food. All the while, I was surprised at how much I was improving. I learned how to recognize a slider. I could see a change-up from a mile away. I was hitting the hard stuff better than ever. I learned to shake off bad days and bad weeks. I had to. I was playing base-ball day in and day out.

Our Auburn team advanced to the playoffs. I desperately wanted to use those extra games to make up for an average season. I did just that. During the five playoff games, I hit .600 and helped our team claim the East Coast League. For the second time in three months, I was a champion.

The season ended and I had a chance to go

home and spend some time with my family. I flew back to San Diego the first week of September. I would be heading to Florida in March for spring training. I had been playing baseball for ten straight months. I was excited to spend some time away from the game.

Before I could catch my breath, my six-month "break" was over. I had to return to Florida for spring training. I had spent much of my break from baseball at home with my family. The rest of the time I was lifting weights and running. I arrived in Vero Beach, Florida in March. Despite being in great shape, nothing prepared me for spring training.

That first spring was less about baseball, and more about survival. I would wake up at 5:15 a.m. and run the obstacle course three times. Then I would do a chest and arm workout routine. Then, I'd run two miles. And this was all before breakfast. After I ate, I would field ground balls at third base. Then I moved on to batting practice. This was everybody's favorite time. We'd laugh, chat, and take huge rips at the ball. Finally, in the afternoon, we'd play a nine-inning game.

At the end of the day, most guys went back to the hotel. I would stick around the field to practice, just like I did in high school. I was determined to make something of my time at camp. The extra practice paid off when I was assigned to play class-A ball in Vero Beach. I had been moved up from rookie ball to high Single-A. This meant I had skipped the Midwestern

League. This was a good sign. I knew that future Major Leaguers would have to jump over levels to reach the "show" during their prime.

Now I only had to survive Vero Beach (Single-A Ball), Amarillo (Double-A Ball) and Cedar Rapids (Triple-A Ball), before I reached Dallas and the Major Leagues. Vero Beach was a huge jump up from rookie ball. The players were much better at the Single-A level. I struggled early on. Slow starts have been a fact of my baseball life. So I wasn't surprised at my .193 average at the midway point of that season.

I was having a hard time in the Florida League for a number of reasons. First of all, I was facing the toughest pitching I'd ever seen. Secondly, I was doing so in front of about twenty-five people per game. In terms of fan support, there was none. Baseball is only as good as its fans. And in Vero Beach, we didn't have any.

In the second half of the season, though, things started to turn around. I got used to empty stadiums and Florida's humidity. I also got used to some of the best pitching in the minors. I hit .288 with 13 home runs during the last seventy games. And for the second straight year, I saved my best performance for the playoffs. I batted .550 in the postseason.

I felt strong when I returned to Vero Beach the next season for my second spring training. Upon my arrival in Florida, executives in the Lonestar organization told me I was playing for a chance to move up to

Double-A. I knew the move to Amarillo would be the most important step on my road to the Majors. By plain percentages alone, my chances of becoming a Major Leaguer were three times better once I reached Amarillo. Only ten percent of Single-A players reach the Majors. That number goes up to thirty percent at the Double-A level.

Spring training went great. A few days before camp broke, I would find out if anyone had taken notice. "Assignment day" was upon us...

And that's where this whole story starts. On "assignment day" in Vero Beach. The day I became a Major League prospect and swirled around on the ocean floor, dreaming.

Chapter 13: The Show

Three days after my surfing accident, I was headed to Amarillo. During my Double-A season, I batted .325 with 28 home runs and 104 RBIs in 140 games. All three totals were career-high marks for me. I even surprised myself. Everything went perfectly and we also qualified for the playoffs.

We survived a series with Reno and would play Ames, Iowa, for the Championship. Behind great starting pitching, we took a three-game-to-one lead. Ames would have to beat us three times in a row.

Ten thousand screaming fans, the largest crowd of the year, packed Amarillo Stadium. They hoped to see their team celebrate a League Championship. Ames took a 3-1 lead in the fourth. The celebration looked like it would have to be put on hold. Then Chad Barnett hit a three-run homer and Kevin Cove hit a two-run shot. Their power surge gave us a three-run lead going into the ninth. When Hector Gomez pumped a fastball by Ames' Mark Tontz, the crowd went nuts. The game was over, and I was a champion—again.

All of the guys stood together behind the pitcher's mound. Coach John Kingman was presented with the League Championship trophy. Coach Kingman grabbed the microphone and thanked the fans for their support.

We all applauded once Coach finished, and began exiting the field. Another year of Minor League baseball had come to a close. The applause came to a halt as Coach Kingman spoke again, "I can't wait to do this again next year." The crowd went into an uproar. Coach went on, "Before we call it a night, I have an announcement. Jimmy Hanks, get over here," Coach had a smile on his face. I moved towards the front of the pitcher's mound. I became nervous right away. What was Coach doing? I had a strong regular season. Maybe he was going to congratulate me. I was uncomfortable with this. The entire team should be recognized, not just me.

Coach looked at me and spoke. "This morning I received a call from the General Manager of the Lonestars, Jake Minnis. He had some super news for you. I wanted to tell you earlier but I was waiting for the right time." The crowd pumped in some more noise. "This feels like the right time, Jimmy."

No way, I thought, there was no chance, it was just not possible that..."You've been called up to the Major Leagues. The Dallas Lonestars. You leave tomorrow. Good luck in 'the show' fella."

Right then, I lost control. I dropped down to my knees and started crying. That was it for me. Everything I had worked for. I was a Major Leaguer. I had received a promotion to the Majors. Next stop, Dallas.

The flight from Amarillo to Dallas was a short one. I arrived the next day in time for batting practice.

We had a 7:00 p.m. game against Pittsburgh. A man wearing a suit with a Lonestars logo on it led me into Lonestar Stadium. After walking through hallway after hallway, we made our way to the clubhouse.

After looking around the room, I had to pick my jaw up off the floor. I had never seen anything like this place. Everything was brand new. I mean every-thing. There was a flat screen television showing last night's highlights. There were leather couches. There was a ping pong table, a sauna, a hot tub, and a buffet with mounds of food. I munched on a piece of chicken. Even the food tasted better in the Majors.

"Your locker is over there," the man pointed to his left. I walked over to my locker. Three Lonestar jerseys hung next to one another. There was a gray one for warm-ups, a blue one for road games, and a white one for home. Socks and pants were folded neatly underneath. I turned my white home jersey around. "Hanks" and the number thirty were written on the back. I laughed out loud. I was really here. There were three freshly carved bats. They were the exact weight and length that I used, waiting for me. Then, I glanced down at two pairs of size twelve cleats. In the Minors, I was always saving money for new cleats. Now I had two new pairs, just my size.

I quickly changed into my warm-up gear and sat down on the chair in front of my locker. I laced up my shiny black cleats and put on a Lonestar cap that fit perfectly. Then I grabbed a pair of bats and ran down a never-ending tunnel.

When I emerged, I was standing on a Major League field. It was the coolest sight ever. As soon as I set foot onto the field, a baseball rolled in front of me. I bent down to pick it up. The ball was brand new. In the Minors, we'd reach into the trash to save a ball. Now I'd be hitting new ones in practice.

I approached the batting cage and saw Major Leaguers pounding baseballs. These were the best hitters I'd ever seen. I recognized all the names on the backs of the jerseys. Some of the guys who I had watched play the game my whole life, were now my teammates. It was a magical feeling.

I didn't get to take a cut in batting practice. After the National Anthem played, I got comfortable on the bench. It was the best seat I'd ever had for a Major League Baseball game. I made a couple of new friends and munched on sunflower seeds. We all clapped and rooted for our team.

As I threw another dozen seeds into my mouth in the   bottom of the eighth inning, I heard a voice at the other end of the dugout.

"Hey, Hanks!" Lonestar Manager Larry Diggs screamed to me.

"Yeah Coach?" I shouted back through a mouthful of seeds.

"Grab yourself a bat, kid! You're on deck."